"We both know we'll be together tonight."

"Mutual attraction," Sierra whispered. A blush stained her smooth alabaster skin, and Ben would have bet anything she'd never come on to a stranger before.

"I'm definitely attracted." He was intrigued, too, and determined to get to the bottom of the puzzle she presented. "Except I'd love some conversation. For me, there's got to be more than lust at first sight."

The pinkish color on her cheeks deepened to a rosy red before she tossed her hair back and held his gaze. The latter looked like an effort for her. "Then tell me about yourself," she asked.

"What do you want to know?"

Her delicate shoulders rose, then fell. "What are you doing in Indigo Springs?"

"Creating memories—good ones, I hope."

Dear Reader,

Five of my relatives are journalists who work for three different daily newspapers. The count would be six if I hadn't abandoned the trade years ago to pursue writing novels. Any one of us could pontificate about the importance of truth. But should the truth always come out?

That question led me to create the character of Ben Nash, who receives an anonymous e-mail that gives him a chance to unlock the decades-old mystery of how his mother died. Ben is an investigative reporter driven to uncover and report the all-important truth. Will the fact that he's falling in love with the daughter of the man who could be responsible for his mother's death change anything?

An Honorable Man is the fourth of the five books in my RETURN TO INDIGO SPRINGS series. I hope you'll enjoy revisiting familiar characters and meeting new ones.

Until next time,

Darlene Gardner

P.S. Visit me on the Web at www.darlenegardner.com.

An Honorable Man
Darlene Gardner

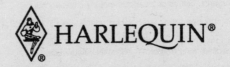

TORONTO • NEW YORK • LONDON
AMSTERDAM • PARIS • SYDNEY • HAMBURG
STOCKHOLM • ATHENS • TOKYO • MILAN • MADRID
PRAGUE • WARSAW • BUDAPEST • AUCKLAND

Recycling programs
for this product may
not exist in your area.

ISBN-13: 978-0-373-71636-4

AN HONORABLE MAN

Copyright © 2010 by Darlene Hrobak Gardner.

www.eHarlequin.com

Printed in U.S.A.

ABOUT THE AUTHOR

While working as a newspaper sportswriter, Darlene Gardner realized she'd rather make up quotes than rely on an athlete to say something interesting. So she quit her job and concentrated on a fiction career that landed her at Harlequin/ Silhouette Books, where she's written for the Temptation, Duets and Intimate Moments lines before finding a home at Superromance. Please visit Darlene on the Web at www.darlenegardner.com.

Books by Darlene Gardner

HARLEQUIN SUPERROMANCE

*Return to Indigo Springs

Don't miss any of our special offers. Write to us at the following address for information on our newest releases.

Harlequin Reader Service
U.S.: 3010 Walden Ave., P.O. Box 1325, Buffalo, NY 14269
Canadian: P.O. Box 609, Fort Erie, Ont. L2A 5X3

To print journalists.
May they survive.

CHAPTER ONE

DO YOU KNOW WHAT really happened to your mother?

Ben Nash stared at the words on the computer screen. Blood rushed to his ears, obliterating the background noise in the *Pittsburgh Tribune* newsroom. It felt as though a vise gripped his heart, stopping his blood from circulating.

His mother had died nineteen years ago in a fall from a cliff in a Pocono Mountain town called Indigo Springs when Ben was twelve years old. He'd always been told it was an accident.

The return address on the e-mail was mountaindweller-blaine@yahoo.com. His mother had never used her married surname of Nash, preferring to be known as Allison Blaine.

He clicked the e-mail closed with a trembling hand and scanned his in-box, identifying a second message from the same sender. The subject header was identical: *Your Mother*. He sucked in a breath and pressed the button on his mouse.

Why wasn't Dr. Ryan Whitmore investigated?

The Whitmore name was unfamiliar, as were most things associated with Indigo Springs aside from pain and loss. Ben's maternal grandparents had retired to the town just months before the ill-fated accident to help friends start up a restaurant. After the tragedy they'd fled Indigo Springs, unable to deal with daily reminders of what had happened.

For Ben, though, the memories were ever present. An image of his mother, with her brown eyes warm with love and her lips curving into a tender smile, was imprinted on his mind as indelibly as an etching.

He checked the date and time at the top right-hand corner of the e-mail. Friday, 9:15 a.m. The second contact had been sent just minutes after the first. A scant hour ago. He hit Reply and typed a message of his own: *Who are you?*

Within moments, the e-mail popped back into his inbox with a Failure Notice heading. He scrolled through it, picking out the words *undeliverable* and *user doesn't have a yahoo.com account.*

"Damn it," he snapped.

"Something wrong, Nash?" Joe Geraldi, the managing editor of the *Tribune,* stood beside Ben's desk.

With a trim build and a full head of prematurely white hair, Joe radiated a brisk energy, the force of which he directed at Ben. It snapped Ben out of his trance. "Where's the IT department?"

Joe screwed up his lean, expressive face. "Geez, Ben. You've worked here for two years and don't know where IT is?"

"I know IT's extension." Technical help was a phone call away, a godsend for a reporter habitually in a rush. This matter, however, needed to be dealt with in person.

"Will you tell me where they are or should I ask someone else?"

"Second floor."

"Thanks." Ben rolled back his chair, got to his feet and strode toward the elevator past cubicles where other reporters talked on phones and typed on computer keyboards.

"Hold up." Joe's raised voice trailed him. "I need to talk to you."

"Sorry. This can't wait." Ben didn't break stride, which wouldn't sit well with Joe. The two of them sometimes grabbed a meal together after working late, but Joe was, above all, his boss. Ben called back over his shoulder, "I'll explain later."

He nearly plowed into the diminutive editor of the business section, muttered a hurried apology and kept going. Bypassing the elevator, he ran lightly down two floors of stairs and emerged on the second floor. It was a neater version of the newsroom, with the piles of paper and files reporters typically kept on their desks largely absent. Flimsy walls separated the workspaces into cubicles. He stopped at the first one, where a young man wearing a long-sleeved T-shirt and jeans hunched over his keyboard.

"Could you help me trace an e-mail?" Ben asked.

The man looked up over his wire-rimmed glasses and leaned back in his chair. He had a shock of dark hair and an unlined, earnest face that communicated amusement. His jaw worked on a piece of gum and Ben got a whiff of spearmint. "First you'll have to tell me who you are."

"Sorry." Ben rubbed the back of his neck, encountering cords of tension. He was often abrupt, but seldom rude. "Ben Nash. I work upstairs."

"Oh, yeah. You wrote the series that ran in Sunday's paper about corruption in the police department. That's bound to shake things up."

The story had consumed Ben for two months, during which he might have averaged six hours of sleep a night, yet at the moment it seemed unimportant. "That's why I wrote it."

"I'm Keith Snyder. We've talked on the phone."

"I recognize the voice." Ben didn't have the patience for any more small talk. "Well, can you do it? Can you trace that e-mail?"

"That's like asking Superman if he can fly." Keith flexed his fingers. "Let me at it."

In a surprisingly short time, most of which Keith spent dispensing insider information about IP addresses and computer networks, Ben had an answer. The e-mail originated from a computer inside the Indigo Springs public library. The air-conditioning suddenly felt as though it had been lowered a few notches.

"Can you narrow it to a specific computer?" Ben asked.

"Afraid not," Keith said. "Could have come from anywhere inside the building, and most libraries have a bank of public access computers."

"How about the e-mail address itself? Any way to check whose account it is?"

"You mean whose account it *was*. I use Yahoo! mail, too." Keith gestured to the mountaindweller-blaine part of the e-mail open on his computer screen. "That dash indicates a disposable address. Seems like it might have been created for one purpose."

"To send to me," Ben said thoughtfully.

"You got it."

"Thanks. I owe you one." Ben clapped him on the shoulder. "I'll buy you a beer after work sometime." That was about the extent of his social activity lately.

"I'll take a rain check." Keith nodded to a photo on his desk of an attractive woman holding a baby dressed entirely in pink, from her shoes to her bonnet. "My wife's on maternity leave. She can't wait for me to get home so I can give her a break."

Nobody was waiting for Ben. He'd gotten the investigative reporting job at the *Tribune* after establishing his name at a series of smaller papers throughout the state. He'd never worked a set schedule or taken the standard weekend days off. The long hours came with the job, as did a burning curiosity. Keith had focused on the technical aspects of the e-mail, completely ignoring the content, a feat that would have been impossible for Ben.

His boss *would* ask questions, something Ben anticipated when he returned to the newsroom and rapped on the frame of the open door to the managing editor's corner office.

"If you hadn't just broken a story, I'd fire your ass," Joe said from behind his desk. Through the window behind him, gray clouds hovered above the city buildings and the visible part of the Monongahela River, emitting a misty drizzle that made it difficult to tell it was spring.

"Never happen," Ben said. "I'm your most valuable asset."

"My most valuable asset is gonna find himself covering the dog show down at the convention center if he doesn't watch his back."

"Can't do it," Ben said. "I need some time off."

A deep furrow appeared between Joe's brows. "Impossible. I just got a tip about a group home for the mentally ill that's kicking out residents left and right. Something's not right at this place. That's what I wanted to talk to you about."

"Normally, I'm your guy, Joe. But not this time. I really need that time off."

"For what?"

Ben hesitated. "It's personal."

Joe crossed his arms over his chest, dislodging one side of his blue dress shirt. It came untucked by the end of almost every workday. "Then let me personally assure you that you're not getting squat unless you start talking."

Sighing heavily, Ben walked to the door and pulled it shut. "You can be a real jerk, did you know that?"

"That's what my ex-wife always says but she doesn't work for me. You do."

Ben leaned with his back against the closed door, pretending a calm he didn't feel. "It's my mother. I just got some e-mails about her."

"I thought your mother died a long time ago."

Ben swallowed. "She did."

While Ben divulged the content of the e-mails and IT's findings, Joe got out of his chair and circled the desk. He perched on the edge of the piece of heavy furniture, all his intensity focused on Ben. "You never told me what happened to her."

"It was an accident, or so I was told. She took me and my two brothers to visit her parents in this little town in the Poconos. One night she went to one of those lookouts with the scenic views and she fell."

"One *night?* Why would she go to a lookout at night?"

Ben had never received a satisfactory answer to that question or the numerous others he'd asked his father over the years. Even though Ben had always felt there was more to his mother's death than he'd been told, his father wasn't the best source. He hadn't even been present in Indigo Springs when his wife died.

"I don't think it was fully dark yet. She had a camera with her so supposedly she was there to take photos," Ben said, although that theory had never seemed quite right. His mother had kept photo albums, but they were dominated by snapshots of family members smiling into the camera, not scenery. "It's time I found out the whole story. At the very least I want to know who sent those e-mails and why they waited twenty years."

Joe remained silent for a long time. Outside the weather had worsened, and Ben could hear the patter of rain on the windowpanes. Indigo Springs was in the Pocono Mountains on the other side of the state, a drive of five to six hours. If he went directly home and packed a bag, he could be there by mid- to late-afternoon.

"If you want the time off, you got it," Joe finally said. "Let me run something by you first. It's okay if you don't want to do it."

"Do what?" Ben asked warily.

"Write a story from the angle of an investigative reporter uncovering the mystery of his mother's death. On the clock, of course."

Ben felt his muscles bunch. "Why would I do that?"

"Because I know you, Ben. Writing's cathartic. It'd be a way for you to deal with the past once and for all." He hesitated, as though unsure whether to continue. Finally, he did. "Not to mention it'd make a really good story."

Joe's argument had merit. Ben totally engrossed himself in a story until it came out in print. Only then could he let it go. Maybe Joe was right. Maybe writing the story would exorcise his demons.

"What about that tip?" Ben realized he'd just agreed to his boss's proposition.

"I'll have Larry Timmons look in to it." Joe named an ambitious reporter who had assisted Ben on a few occasions, a young guy hungry to get ahead—Larry reminded Ben of himself. "He's been hounding me for a chance to take the lead on a big story."

It went against Ben's makeup to put anyone else in the driver's seat, let alone somebody who would fight not to give up the wheel. "Maybe what I need to do won't take long."

Joe snorted softly. "With a rottweiler, it usually doesn't."

"Excuse me?"

"Rottweiler," Joe repeated. "That's what the other reporters call you."

Ben hadn't been aware he had a nickname. "Do I want to know why?"

"Once you sink your teeth in a story, you don't let go." Joe seemed to relish in the telling. "That Dr. Whitmore doesn't stand a chance."

CHAPTER TWO

DR. SIERRA WHITMORE turned away from her reflection in the gift-shop window too late to avoid the image of the long, caramel-brown hair she'd been too chicken to part with.

"Just a trim, please," she muttered to herself.

That's what she'd requested when the hip, young stylist who was the new hire at her hair salon asked if she was feeling adventurous. Her intention to have her hair cut boy-short never made it past her lips.

Sierra fished a tie out of her purse and hastily pulled her hair into a loose twist, the way she usually wore it, silently berating herself all the while for her stunning lack of courage.

"Hello, Dr. Whitmore."

The greeting pulled Sierra out of her daze. The woman passing her on the sidewalk in the heart of the picturesque downtown of Indigo Springs was a patient at the practice where Sierra worked in partnership with her brother.

"Good day, Mrs. Jorgenson."

The woman gave her a tepid smile and kept walking. *Good day.*

Had Sierra really just said that? The woman was roughly her age. She should have uttered a casual hello and addressed her by her first name, like a normal person would have done.

It was time she faced up to the terrible truth her ex-boyfriend, Chad Armstrong, had slammed her with when he broke up with her last month.

She was boring.

Mind-numbingly, nobody's-in-a-rut-deeper-than-I-am boring.

Even more dull than Chad himself, who could kill a conversation with his pharmacist shoptalk when he bothered to say anything at all.

If the charge wasn't true, she'd be headed out of town to meet an old college friend for a wild weekend of clubbing. She'd have asked her brother to cover for her rather than refusing the invitation because she was on call.

She didn't have any firm plans for this weekend at all, which was why she was heading back to the office. Even when Whitmore Family Practice closed early, as it did every Friday afternoon, Sierra could always find some paperwork.

She spotted a flyer advertising next weekend's Indigo Springs Arts and Music Festival alongside a splashy modern painting in the window of an art studio. The other tourist-themed businesses on the pretty, hilly street—restaurants, bike and ski shops, souvenir stores—sported similar notices. She was wondering why a banner promoting the event hadn't been strung over Main Street, when she saw the man.

He wore dark shades even though the sun wasn't particularly bright. In a short-sleeved black polo shirt that stretched across his broad shoulders, he was seemingly oblivious to the slight chill typical of the latter part of April. The section of sidewalk where he stood with his hands shoved in the pockets of his jeans was shaded by a red maple tree, its vibrant leaves forming a backdrop that caused him to appear ridiculously masculine. The smell of flowers in bloom wafted on a breeze, a further contradiction.

She snuck a glance at him as she approached, appreciating the sensuous line of his mouth, the wave in his thick dark hair and his solid build. He looked to have three days' growth of beard, which somehow made him seem more sexy. So did his height. She judged him to be at least six feet two, maybe even six-three.

"Excuse me." The timbre of his voice, soft and deep and without an accent she could detect, reached out to her. "Sorry to bother you, but can you recommend a place to stay?"

That meant he was a visitor, unsurprising in a place marketed as a year-round tourist destination. Besides, if this man lived in Indigo Springs, she would have noticed him before now.

"Try the Blue Stream Bed-and-Breakfast. It's up the street a few blocks." She pointed to indicate the direction. "If that's full, I'd give the Indigo Inn a shot. It's back the other way."

"Have you stayed at either of those places?" he asked.

"No, I haven't. Some locals book a room at the

B and B just to sample the blueberry scones the owner serves for breakfast, but so far I've resisted."

"So you live here in Indigo Springs?"

She wished he wasn't wearing those shades so she could see whether the color of his eyes complemented his long, straight nose and strong jawline, which was partially obscured by dark stubble. "I do."

"Can you steer me toward me a good place for dinner tonight?"

"Can I ever." She gestured across the street to a Thai restaurant with a bright red door. "That place has the best pad thai I've ever had. It's so good I could eat it every day of the week."

He didn't hesitate. "Then how about having pad thai tonight? With me."

The breeze cooled the interior of Sierra's mouth, alerting her that it must have dropped open. "You want me to have dinner with you?" she repeated, just in case she'd misunderstood.

"Sure. Why not? You could save me from eating alone."

A thrill traveled through Sierra before reason took over. "Thank you, but I can't."

"Are you married?" he asked.

"Well, no."

"Engaged?" He didn't give her a chance to answer. "In a relationship? Wary of strange men who approach you on the street?"

She laughed. "No to the first two questions. Yes to the third."

"Not much I can do about that." He gave a small

shrug, emphasizing the play of muscles in his shoulders. "Thanks for the recommendations."

He started walking in the direction of the B and B, leaving Sierra exactly where she'd been before the unforeseen encounter: chiding herself for allowing her life to turn stale.

So what had she done the first time she got the opportunity to do the unexpected?

She'd let her unexpected opportunity get away.

"Wait!" She followed up on her cry by pursuing the stranger. He turned, those eyes still covered by shades, the quirk of his sensuous mouth the only thing betraying his curiosity.

"Are *you* married?" she asked.

"Never been." He lifted a left hand bare of rings. The base of his hand was broad, his fingers long, his knuckles lightly dusted with hair.

Lots of married men didn't wear the evidence, yet she could tell instinctively that he really was single. Chad, with his roots in Indigo Springs and stable job, was the type of guy you could settle down with. Her father had told her that all the time. He'd warn her against this man. Because this man was the kind you took to bed. She fought not to blush at the thought and asked, "What's your name?"

"Ben Nash."

It suited him, strong and to the point, like the man himself.

"Mine's Sierra." She started to add the Whitmore surname, then caught sight of the sign above the doctor's office. Sierra had worked hard to get where she was, but she longed for this man to treat her like a woman, not a physician. He had no notion she'd developed into the biggest bore who'd ever lived.

"Hello, Sierra." He stuck out one of his strong hands, which immediately engulfed hers in warmth, sending a shivery sensation through her. "I guess this means we're not strangers anymore."

That had been her intention. She was through standing back and letting life pass her by. Earlier today she'd wondered how to dig herself out of her rut.

Now she knew.

"I can't make it for dinner." She tried lowering her voice to a flirtatious murmur. "Would you like to meet for drinks instead?"

SIERRA SMOOTHED her hands over the tight jeans that hugged her body like denim Saran Wrap, glimpsed down at the deep, daring vee of her clinging black top and fought the impulse to sprint to her bedroom closet.

She didn't think she moved, but her spike heels were so high she wobbled a little anyway.

The outfit was hers, but she'd only worn the shirt before and always under a sweater. With her straight brown hair taking a free fall down her back, she felt like a stranger.

"Who do I think I'm fooling?" Sierra muttered. Ben Nash had seen how conservatively she was dressed when they met that afternoon. He wouldn't fall for her seductress act tonight.

If, that is, she managed to keep the date.

She shook off the thought. Of course she intended

to meet him. A quick glance at the alarm clock on her bedside table showed she still had twenty minutes until they were scheduled to get together. If she was quick about changing her clothes, she'd barely be late.

She sat down on her bed, crossed one leg over the other and started to pull off her shoe. A rapping sound stopped her.

She went still, listening intently. The tapping stopped, then started again, sounding exactly like a knock. She rolled her eyes. Of course it was a knock. That was how visitors announced their presence in the absence of a doorbell, which the downtown town house she'd moved into last week didn't have.

She crossed the hardwood of her second-floor bedroom, which still smelled of the polish she'd used to bring out its shine, hoping her heels didn't damage the floor. She peeked out the window that faced Main Street. Annie Sublinski Whitmore stood on the doorstep, wearing jeans that fit much looser than Sierra's, a green Indigo River Rafters windbreaker and tennis shoes. Her pickup truck was parked at the curb.

Regretting that she hadn't had time to change her clothes, Sierra headed for the stairs. She gripped the banister to keep from counterbalancing in the unfamiliar heels, made it to the foyer and let Annie into the town house.

"Hope you don't mind me stopping by like…" Annie's voice abruptly lost steam, and her easy-to-read eyes widened. "Wow!"

Sierra grimaced and crossed her arms over her midsection. "It's too much, isn't it?"

"Too much for what?" Annie asked, pulling the door shut behind her.

Sierra hesitated. Annie had become her sister-in-law a few months ago when she'd married Sierra's brother Ryan. The two women had attended high school together once upon a time but they were still working on becoming friends. "I'm meeting someone for drinks."

"Great!" Annie patted the stray hairs the wind had blown loose from her blond ponytail back into place. Her face, devoid of makeup, glowed with natural color from the sun and the wind. "Anyone I know?"

"No."

Annie waited a beat, but Sierra couldn't very well tell her sister-in-law she was screwing up the courage to lose her inhibitions with a sexy stranger.

"I'm glad you're dating again." Annie had a sincerity about her that made everything she said appear genuine. "Really glad."

"Thank you." Sierra's response sounded wooden when she'd meant to communicate how touched she was by Annie's enthusiasm. Suppressing a sigh of frustration, she gestured toward the kitchen at the back of the town house. "Can I get you something to drink?"

"Oh, no," Annie said. "I wouldn't dream of keeping you, and I'm itching to get home to Ryan anyway."

Annie was referring to Sierra's childhood home, a large Colonial in the residential area immediately adjacent to downtown Indigo Springs. Sierra had lived in the house as an adult, too, until deciding the newlyweds should have it to themselves. Annie and Ryan wouldn't be alone for long. At the end of the school year, the daughter they'd given up for adoption when they were teenagers and reconnected with last summer was moving in with them permanently.

"Ryan played pick-up basketball tonight, so I had dinner with my dad after I got off the river." Annie ran a tourist-themed business with her father that offered whitewater trips and mountain bike rentals. "He texted a little while ago that he has a glass of red wine waiting for me."

"Sounds like you deserve to relax." Sierra shifted from high heel to high heel. She was already taller than average. In the shoes, she towered over Annie. "Ryan says you've been working a lot lately."

"Spring's our busiest season, especially when we get a lot of rain. The rafting's terrific when the river's high. We're booking so many trips I won't have time for anything but work the next couple weeks."

"That's good, right?"

"Good for business. Not so good for the festival, which brings me to the reason I stopped by." Annie's long pause was uncharacteristic. "I was hoping you'd fill in for me on the planning committee."

"Me?" Sierra resisted the urge to take a giant step backward, away from the request.

"I know it's a lot to ask, with Chad being a member." Annie made a face. "I thought you might be uncomfortable around him, but Ryan says you're made of tougher stuff than that."

Her brother didn't know her nearly as well as he thought he did.

Sierra pressed her lips together, so she wouldn't

give in to the temptation to refuse outright, and composed an answer. "Do I have to let you know right now?"

"Oh, no." Annie shook her head. "Take a day to think about it. There's a meeting Sunday afternoon and then things'll get pretty busy, especially come festival weekend."

Sierra nodded, hating herself for letting the thought of dealing with her ex-boyfriend stop her from agreeing to help the community. At this rate, Annie would have a hard time warming up to her.

"You'd be a great help to the committee, not to mention you'd be doing me a huge favor," Annie said. "And who knows? After tonight, being on the committee might not seem like such a big deal."

Sierra cocked her head. "What do you mean by after tonight?"

"You're dating again, right?" Annie grinned at her, then let herself out of the town house. Before she pulled the door shut, she stuck her head around the frame.

"One more thing," she said, eyes sparkling. "If you're looking to impress that guy you're meeting, don't you dare change out of those clothes."

BEN STOPPED WATCHING the entrance to the Blue Haven Pub fifteen minutes after Sierra was due to arrive. She'd stood him up, not that it came as a shock.

Sierra had been as skittish as an anonymous source when they'd met even as she tried to project a worldliness he'd seen right through. She was classy, from the toes of her low-heeled pumps to the tailored cut of her blazer to the subtle smell of her perfume. She wasn't the type of woman who arranged dates with strange men.

He fought back disappointment even though he couldn't fault Sierra's judgment. His motives weren't exactly pure. He'd intended to subtly press her for information on the town's inhabitants and find out what she knew about Dr. Whitmore.

Now that he wasn't distracted by her imminent arrival, nothing was stopping him from striking up conversations with the patrons. There were plenty of them, sitting on stools around the bar, playing pool in the back room, gathered around tables hoisting mugs of beer. The pub seemed to be the town's ultimate gathering spot, a place frequented by both locals and tourists.

He imagined his mother sitting in this same bar, perhaps at this very table, unaware she didn't have long to live. A chill penetrated his skin, and he realized his hand had tightened around his frosted glass. He relaxed his grip. His chances of discovering the truth about how his mother had died would be greater if he could treat this like any other story.

So far he hadn't learned much.

The teenage clerk at his hotel had recently moved to town with his family and was unfamiliar with Whitmore Family Practice. The waitress at the Thai restaurant knew only that Ryan Whitmore was a doctor.

Neither had Ben made headway on tracking down the sender of the e-mails. He'd visited the public library at five-thirty that afternoon only to find out it closed at five.

He wished he'd done more groundwork on the

Whitmore family before leaving Pittsburgh. After receiving those anonymous e-mails, however, all he could think about was traveling to where the scent was strongest.

He'd counted on a quick search of the Web yielding all he needed to know. He hadn't anticipated his hotel wouldn't have Internet access and that the only Internet café in town wasn't scheduled to open until next month.

He was about to leave the table and head for an old-timer bellying up to the bar when he caught sight of a woman with long, sexy brown hair at the entrance. She took off her black jacket, revealing clothes that showed off her killer body.

She scanned the interior of the bar, her posture as rigid as that of a mannequin in a store window. She looked in his general direction, and her chest expanded, as though she was sucking in a deep breath. He watched as she ventured forward, curious to see if she'd be joining a lucky guy.

Her steps faltered, but she kept coming in his general direction, navigating the labyrinth of tables, dodging a woman who abruptly stood up. She didn't stop until she drew even with his table and slipped into the chair across from him.

"Hey," she said. "Sorry I'm late."

He was the lucky guy.

He blinked, then blinked again. She had the same high cheekbones, delicate chin and full mouth as the woman he'd met earlier that afternoon. While that Sierra had been pretty in an understated way, this one was a knockout.

"No apology necessary." He kept his eyes trained on

her face instead of indulging himself and letting them dip to the generous cleavage her low-cut shirt displayed. She had the bone structure of a model without the emptiness he perhaps unfairly associated with the excessively beautiful. That term didn't exactly apply to Sierra, mostly because of the intelligence in her eyes, but partly due to a nose that wasn't completely straight. In his opinion, that small imperfection made her more appealing. "You're definitely worth the wait."

"Exactly the reaction I was aiming for." The comment should have sounded flirtatious, but her voice shook slightly, as though she was...nervous?

A middle-aged waitress in a hurry stopped by their table to take Sierra's drink order. Sierra hesitated, then said, "Whiskey."

"Neat?" the waitress asked.

Sierra's eyebrows, finely arched and a shade darker than her hair, drew together. "Excuse me?"

Ben hid a grin and supplied, "Without a mixer."

"Oh, no." Sierra waved a hand airily, as though she ordered whiskey every day of the week. "I like it with water. On the rocks."

Ben waited until the waitress had gone, then set about trying to put her at ease. "The B and B was booked, but I got a room at the Indigo Inn. I also took your advice about the pad thai. It was delicious." He smiled. "The pad thai, I mean. I haven't tasted the room."

"I'm glad." She fidgeted with her gold bracelet, her expression serious. His joke had been lame, but he'd at least expected her to return his smile.

One beat of silence stretched to two, then three.

"So, Sierra whatever-your-last-name-is," he said, "what am I allowed to know about you?"

She stopped playing with the bracelet and clasped her hands primly in her lap, the kind of reaction he might have expected if he'd asked for the pin number of her ATM card.

"I'm not all that interesting," she said.

The understatement of the year, and Ben's years were packed with intriguing things. "Let me be the judge of that."

The waitress saved her from replying by returning with her whiskey, which she set in front of Sierra with a plop before bustling away. Sierra picked up the glass and took a large swallow. Her lips curled and her eyes watered.

Those damp eyes zeroed in on him. "Can we not do this?"

"Do what?"

She waved a slim, pretty hand. Her nails were unpainted. "Pretend to be interested in each other's lives. We both know why we got together tonight."

They did? She shifted in her chair, as though waiting for him to say something. For the life of him, he didn't know what. He wasn't ready to confess his hope that she could tell him about Dr. Whitmore.

"Mutual attraction," she whispered. A blush stained her smooth alabaster skin, and he would have bet his laptop computer she'd never come on to a stranger before.

"I'm definitely attracted." He was intrigued, too, and determined to get to the bottom of the puzzle she presented. "Except I'd love some conversation. For me, there's got to be more than lust at first sight."

The pinkish color on her cheeks deepened to a deep rose before she tossed her hair back and met his eyes. She held his gaze, it looked like with an effort. "Then tell me about *yourself*."

"What do you want to know?"

Her delicate shoulders rose, then fell. "What are you doing in Indigo Springs?"

"Reliving memories." He'd eventually tell her he was an investigative reporter, but the moment wasn't right. "I was here one time as a child. It seemed past time I came back." Something stopped him from revealing his grandparents had once been residents of Indigo Springs. "How about you? Have you lived here long?"

"All my life." She fidgeted and snuck a not-so-covert glance at the people around them. She'd been doing that a lot since she arrived.

"Something wrong?" he asked.

She didn't answer immediately, then finally whispered, "People are staring at us."

"They're staring at *you*," he corrected.

She crossed her arms over her chest and ran her hands up and down the bare skin of her upper arms. "Because they've never seen me dressed like this."

"Because you look fantastic," he countered.

She shook her head, uncrossed her arms, ran a hand over her mouth, then lowered her voice another half octave. "I don't know what I was thinking, coming here tonight."

"I'm not sure what you mean," he said. "We're just two people having a drink together."

"It's more than that." She leaned forward so only he could hear. He could smell something light and flowery. Not perfume, like he'd thought earlier today. Scented shampoo. "I was going to try to get you to invite me back to your room."

His heartbeat sped up to a gallop. "You wouldn't have to try very hard."

"Except I changed my mind." The corners of her mouth drooped. "It's pretty clear I'm not cut out for one-night stands."

The gallop slowed to a trot. He blew out a breath, fighting the compulsion to disagree. "Why did you think you were?"

"It's a long story."

"I've got all night." Pumping her for information about Dr. Whitmore could wait. He looked around for their waitress, didn't find her and nodded at her barely touched whiskey. "I'm having another beer. Want me to get you something else?"

"A diet soda, please," she said primly.

"Coming right up." Pretending he didn't feel as though he'd just lost a jackpot, he maneuvered through a maze of tables to the bar and placed his order.

The bartender was an attractive woman with curly black hair, huge, dark eyes and a warm smile. She could have been anywhere from twenty-five to thirty-five. With quick efficiency, she poured the soda, refilled his beer and set the drinks in front of him. "So how do you know the doc?"

"What doc?" Ryan asked.

She gestured to Sierra with her index finger, the funky bracelets she wore jangling together. "Dr. Whitmore. She looks fantastic tonight, not that she doesn't usually. I just never saw her dress like that before."

Shock momentarily squeezed Ben's windpipe. He hid his astonishment the best he could, swallowed, then muttered the blandest response he could think of. "Mutual friends."

He picked up his beer mug, his brain whirring. It seemed a fantastic coincidence until he noted he'd run across Sierra in the same block as Whitmore Family Practice. The office had been closed, but she must have been returning to the office, perhaps to finish up some work.

He examined her with new eyes en route to the table, putting her age at around thirty, probably just a little younger than he was. She could be Dr. Ryan Whitmore's youthful wife, except she'd claimed not to be married. Was she his daughter?

Excitement flared. No matter how it had happened, he'd stumbled across a delicious opportunity to fill in the many blanks he had about Dr. Ryan Whitmore.

He closed in on Sierra, then noticed her face go white. He followed the direction of her gaze to the bar entrance. A slender man about his age of average height with blond hair receding at the temples nodded in Sierra's direction. She inclined her head slightly, then gazed down at the table.

Her eyes didn't raise until Ben took a seat across from her. They looked big and sad. He cursed inwardly, and the flame of exhilaration he felt when he discovered her last name extinguished.

He was not about to interrogate a woman as fragile as this one about Dr. Ryan Whitmore until he got some other questions answered.

"That long story you were going to tell me, does it have anything to do with that guy?" Ben indicated the new arrival with a slight jerk of his head.

She started. "How did you know that?"

"Lucky guess," Ben said, although his deduction had more to do with powers of observation. "Here's another. He's the ex-boyfriend."

Her chin trembled, and she nodded. "He called it off last month."

"That's rough," he said. "Were you together long?"

"We've known each other since high school, but didn't start dating until I was out of college."

"Sounds serious."

She snuck a look at her ex, then spoke in a voice so soft it was hard to hear. "Everybody thought we'd get married. My father treated him like a son."

"So you were in love with him?"

She didn't answer for so long he thought she regretted what she'd already revealed. Then, finally, she spoke. "I thought so. Now I'm not so sure. He's solid and dependable, but set in his ways."

"Ah," Ben said as understanding dawned. "Is one of his routines coming to the Blue Haven on Friday nights?"

Guilt flitted across her face. "He's here on Tuesdays and on Fridays, never for longer than an hour. He always orders mineral water with a twist of lime."

"Sounds boring."

"Funny you should use that word. He broke up with me because he said *I* was boring." She crossed her arms over her midsection. "He may be right, too. I just proved it all over again with you."

"Because you're passing up that chance to have your way with me?" He made his eyebrows dance, coaxing the hint of a grin from her pretty bowed lips.

"Yes." She cast another surreptitious glance at her ex-boyfriend, and the partial grin vanished. "No offense, but I'm calling it a night. Please don't feel like you have to leave, too."

"I can at least walk you out." No way would he let her face her ex alone and vulnerable if he could help it. He pushed back from the table, then waited for her to precede him.

She put on her jacket and kept her eyes forward as they moved together toward the exit. The other man sat in a booth beside a window that afforded a view of the street. He stared at them intently, his gaze following them even after they were outside in the cool night air.

Ben stopped on the sidewalk and faced Sierra, careful to stay in her ex-boyfriend's sight line. "I take it you met me tonight so your ex could see us together?"

She grimaced, her slightly crooked nose crinkling. "Partly. And partly to prove to myself I could be unpredictable." She gazed heavenward, then down again. "Except neither of those worked out so well."

"They could," he said. "Your ex is awfully interested in what we're doing out here."

"We're not doing anything," she said.

"We will be." He advanced a step and gathered her into his arms. Before she could stiffen, he whispered, "Relax or it won't look realistic."

She blinked up at him. "What won't look realistic?"

"The show we're going to give him."

He half expected her to yank out of his arms, but she surprised him, relaxing her body so she appeared less tense than at any other time tonight. He could smell the light floral scent he now knew was her shampoo mixed with the warmth of her skin as her soft curves molded against him. A glint of mischievousness appeared in her eyes. "Do you think we can pull it off?"

"Oh, yeah." He winked at her, then dipped his head.

Her lips molded to his in the sweetest of kisses, her arms twining around his neck to pull him close. He angled his body and gathered her intimately against him so her jerk of an ex-boyfriend could get an eyeful.

Their embrace confirmed what he already knew: Her ex was an idiot. Nothing was remotely boring about a woman who could kiss like this.

She might have been pretending, but it was a good act. She was tall for a woman, especially in her spiked heels, but felt delicate in his arms. He threaded his fingers through her luxurious long hair, which felt like silk against his skin. Her lips clung to his, her tongue darting out to stroke the tip of his. He accepted her invitation, letting his tongue slide inside her mouth.

He'd kissed a lot of women in his thirty-one years but never did he remember a first kiss like this. Their mouths melded, their bodies fit, their hearts seemed to beat in tandem. His arousal was instantaneous.

A rumble echoed in his ears, which he attributed to the blood roaring through his veins. A shrill staccato noise blared. A car horn. Belatedly, he remembered where he was and what he was doing. Correction. What he was *attempting* to convince Sierra he was doing.

Putting on a show. With a relative of the man who might have been involved in his mother's death, no less.

He pulled back, his mouth reluctantly parting from hers. Her green eyes appeared huge as they stared back at his. He cleared his throat. "Well, I'll say we fooled him."

She nodded, appearing dazed. "Yeah."

He disengaged from her, struggling to get his body under control, although she couldn't miss the effect she'd had on him. He tried to make his voice sound natural. "Let me walk you to your car."

"That's not necessary." Her voice sounded low and shaky. "I only live a few blocks away."

"Then I'll walk you home."

She seemed about to protest further, then closed her mouth and nodded. They walked the next few blocks in silence, not touching, a half body length separating them. The street got quieter as businesses gradually gave way to a quaint row of town houses with stone facades.

"It's this one." She stopped in front of one of the more classy residences. A wrought-iron railing led to a redbrick door. A pot of colorful flowers adorned the ledge protruding from the front window. The entire home emanated grace and beauty, like its owner. She tucked a strand of her long hair behind her ear, which struck him as sensual. Then again, at this point just about every move she made was sexy. "Thank you for what you did back there at the bar."

He nearly laughed aloud. "Believe me, it was my pleasure."

Her cheeks colored, charming him all over again. He lightly rubbed the back of his knuckles against the stain, then pulled his hand back. He knew better than to reach for her again.

"You know what I wish?" he asked softly.

She stared up at him with her big eyes, her head shaking back and forth so that silken hair of hers swayed.

"I wish you were the kind of woman who indulged in one-night stands," he said.

She anchored her hands on his shoulders, stood on tiptoe and kissed him, so briefly it was just an electric brushing of lips.

"Me, too." She spoke so close to his mouth he felt her warm breath and smelled the faintest trace of whiskey. "Goodbye, Ben Nash."

She disappeared inside, leaving him staring at the closed door. Only then did he realize that neither of them had thought to check her ex-boyfriend's reaction to their kiss.

Resigned to an early night, he headed in the direction of his downtown hotel. If he meant to preserve the fiction he and Sierra had just created, returning to the Blue Haven wasn't an option.

The real world would intrude soon enough, because the two wishes he'd kept to himself had no better chance of coming true than the first.

That Sierra's last name wasn't Whitmore.

And that tomorrow morning he wouldn't have to break the news to her that he was an investigative reporter.

CHAPTER THREE

THE SPINACH AND CHEESE omelet at Jimmy's Diner was every bit as delicious as Sierra had always heard. So was the coffee: thick, rich and not bitter in the slightest.

"Can I get anything else for you, Doc?" Ellie Marson, the waitress who was as much a mainstay at Jimmy's as the red vinyl booths, bustled over to Sierra on Saturday morning. If Sierra hadn't noticed her birth date when Ellie was in the office a few months ago complaining of foot pain, she'd never have guessed the other woman was sixty-two.

"Just the check, please," Sierra said.

"Coming right up." Ellie quickly shuffled through the orders on her pad and ripped off a sheet. "I never did thank you for referring me to that podiatrist."

"Did he take care of the problem?" Sierra asked.

The waitress pointed to the pair of white thick-soled shoes on her feet. "These did the trick. Would have told you sooner if you'd come in here for breakfast before today."

"I usually eat at home," Sierra said.

Who was she kidding? She *always* started the day

with a glass of orange juice and a low-fat, high-fiber cereal consumed at her own kitchen table. She'd complained about Chad Armstrong slavishly following his routines, yet the only thing she varied was whether she filled her bowl with Frosted Mini-Wheats or Special K.

Until today, when she'd awakened remembering the way Ben Nash had looked at her last night.

If she could attract the attention of a dynamic man like Ben simply by being a little more daring, it was time to act a lot less predictably.

So she'd gone for a brisk early-morning walk instead of popping in her customary exercise DVD and skipped her cereal for the specialty omelet at Jimmy's Diner. She'd even dug through a closet containing mostly pastels and neutral colors and pulled out her lone red top, which she'd paired with a flirty navy skirt a few inches shorter than the ones she usually wore.

"Well, I sure am glad you decided to stop in this morning," the waitress said. "I'd love to see you here more often."

"Thanks, Ms. Mar…" Sierra stopped herself, remembering her vow to loosen up. This was someone she'd known for years. "I mean, Ellie."

"No need to thank me for speaking the truth," Ellie said. "It does a body good to work less and the soul to eat out more, 'cept next time you should eat at the counter."

She'd make a note of that, Sierra thought as Ellie went off to wait on another customer. The other solo diners had opted to sit where they could interact. Sierra knew a fair number of the customers, although none of them well, including the tall brunette who reached the exit at the same time she did. Sierra held the door open.

"Thanks." Sara Brenneman held a foam cup of take-out coffee in each hand. A lawyer who lived and worked in the block adjacent to Sierra's town house, Sara was dressed in jeans and a windbreaker instead of the smart, stylish business clothes she favored. Her windbreaker, however, was hot-pink. "I was just talking about you this morning."

Sierra felt her cheeks grow warm despite a temperature that probably hadn't yet hit sixty. Had Sara been at the Blue Haven last night? Had she seen Sierra leave the bar with Ben Nash? Had she witnessed the kiss?

"I called Annie this morning about festival business and she said you might take her place on the committee," Sara explained.

Sierra relaxed. "I'm thinking about it."

"Think fast because we need the help, not to mention Annie says you'd be great at it." Sara walked quickly and purposefully down the sidewalk even though they were heading more than slightly uphill, past shops and restaurants not yet open for business. On a Saturday morning, the town was slow to wake up. "If you decide to fill in, the meeting's tomorrow at Quincy Coleman's house."

"Really? Quincy Coleman?" Sierra wondered if Annie had purposely neglected to mention who was hosting the meeting. Surely she was aware that the retired banker's one-sided feud with her late father hadn't endeared him to the rest of the Whitmore family.

"I was surprised when I found out he was on the committee, too," Sara said. "He's been unexpectedly easy to deal with. He seems to be trying to make amends for the past."

Coleman's most egregious offense was unfairly holding Michael Donahue, Sara's fiancé, responsible for the death of his daughter. Taking potshots at Sierra's father whenever the opportunity presented itself paled in comparison.

"Anyway, I hope to see you at the meeting," she said. "Oh. And I almost forgot. Annie says you have a friend in Harrisburg who owns a bridal shop. I'd love her business card, if you have one."

"Does that mean you and Michael have set a date?"

Sara beamed, her entire face lighting up even though the sun was rising at her back. "The last Saturday in June."

"And you don't have your dress yet?"

"Now you sound just like Annie," Sara said in a long-suffering voice. "Two months is plenty of time."

Not if the dress needed alterations, it wasn't.

"I'll be sure to get you that card," Sierra said.

"Great." The lawyer left Sierra with a smile, then immediately picked up her pace, no doubt eager to rejoin her fiancé. Sierra wondered if Sara served Michael Donahue coffee in bed and had a pang that she'd passed up the chance to do the same for Ben Nash.

Ben Nash, who was passing through town and who she'd probably never see again.

Before regret could take hold, she focused on the morning ahead. Unlike many other family physicians, she and Ryan didn't start the morning with hospital rounds. Because of time and distance constraints, it made more sense to use hospitalists—specialists who provided care to patients while they were in the hospital. She let herself into the medical practice through the back entrance and was shrugging into her lab coat when Missy Cromartie rushed down the hall.

"Dr. Sierra, am I glad you're here!" Missy was short and slight with large eyes that nearly overwhelmed her pretty, elfin face. Her dramatic coloring, black hair and blue eyes set in pale skin, suited her personality. "When I got to work ten minutes ago, a man was waiting outside to see Dr. Ryan. I told him to come back at nine when we opened, but he wanted to come in and wait."

"You did fine, Missy." Sierra gentled her voice to calm the excitable receptionist. "It's okay if he waits inside."

"You don't understand." If possible, Missy's light-colored eyes grew larger and rounder. Her shoulder-length hair shook along with her head. "He doesn't have an appointment."

"I'm sure you can squeeze him in."

"But he's not sick! I tried telling him how busy it gets on Saturdays, but he said he'll wait as long as it takes. I don't know what to do with him."

Sierra started to tell Missy to handle the problem the best she could, then thought better of it. That's what the old Sierra would say. The new Sierra met challenges head-on…if she didn't count her reluctance to join the festival committee.

"Would you like me to talk to him?" Sierra asked.

"That'd be great!" Missy's relief was out of proportion to the offer. "Just great!"

Sierra plastered on a professional smile, walked purposefully toward the waiting room and froze. Her heart did a leap worthy of the basketball players she liked to watch on television. The man sitting in the middle of a bank of chairs against the serene backdrop of a blue wall wasn't just any man.

It was Ben Nash.

"Ben!" she cried.

His eyes lifted from the pages of *Newsweek,* his face reflecting none of the surprise she felt certain was on her own. Her mind darted in a dozen directions while her heart pounded. She shouldn't be happy to see him, not when he was nothing more than a passing distraction. Yet she was.

He stood up. "Hello, Sierra."

He was even better-looking this morning, the cream color of his long-sleeve shirt contrasting with his olive skin, his eyes clear. She'd found out last night they were brown, to match his hair. It still appeared as though he hadn't shaved in three days, which must be his usual look. She'd never been partial to facial hair on men, but his stubble added to his rugged good looks.

She advanced, trying to slow down her steps. Missy must have heard him wrong. Ben Nash wasn't waiting to see Sierra's brother: he was here to see her. She felt her smile break free.

"This is a surprise." She stemmed the desire to walk into his arms and stopped a few feet shy of him. "I didn't think I'd see you again."

"I'm sorry I gave you that impression."

That was a strange thing to say. Did he honestly believe she'd hold it against him that he'd been secretly planning to seek her out? But how had he found her? "I know I didn't tell you I was a doctor."

"You didn't have to," he said. "In a town this small, people talk."

For one of the first times in her life, she was glad gossip was a favorite pastime among the locals in Indigo Springs. Otherwise, she might not have had the pleasure of seeing Ben again. Or the chance to find out where what they'd started last night would lead.

"I won't get off work until about one o'clock." She couldn't ask Ryan to take her patient load. They were far too busy on Saturday mornings for one doctor. "Then I'm completely free for the rest of the day."

"I might not be. I'm here on business," he said, something else that didn't make sense.

"Business?" She cocked her head, regarding him quizzically. "What kind of business?"

"I'm a reporter for the *Pittsburgh Tribune*." He cleared his throat, the strong column contracting. "I have reason to believe Dr. Ryan Whitmore can help me with a story."

Missy hadn't misunderstood why Ben had showed up in the office this morning.

Sierra had.

The knowledge slammed into her at the same time the front door swung open to admit her brother, who almost never used the back entrance. He stopped his tuneless whistling, ran a hand through his fair head of wind-tousled hair and gave them an eye-crinkling smile. Since Ryan had married Annie in February, he did a lot of smiling.

"Good morning, sis." A born extrovert, he strode

across the room, stretching out a hand to Ben. "Ryan Whitmore. I don't believe we've met."

Sierra heard Ben's quick intake of breath before he stood and shook her brother's hand. "Ben Nash from the *Pittsburgh Tribune*."

Sierra choked back her disappointment. "Ben's here to talk to you."

"I'm not so sure about that." Ben was gazing at Ryan with open skepticism. "I was expecting Ryan Whitmore to be a much older man."

"I was named after our father," Ryan said. "He died two years ago."

Ben rubbed the back of his neck as Sierra tried to figure out what was going on. Why had a Pittsburgh reporter come to Indigo Springs to talk to a dead man? And why hadn't he told her who he was last night?

"What is this about?" Ryan asked before she could form the question.

"I'm following up on a lead that your father might have information about a woman who died in Indigo Springs," he said.

Yet Ben had failed to tell her any of this the night before. Their "chance" meeting and his invitation to get together suddenly didn't seem accidental. She crossed her arms over her heaving stomach.

The door swung open again. Art Czerbiak, who always insisted on the first appointment of the morning, shuffled through. What was left of the elderly man's gray hair was in disarray from the April wind. He muttered a gruff good-morning and took a seat at the far end of the room, then regarded them with interest.

Missy was also watching them closely, not even trying to disguise her stares.

"The waiting room isn't the best place to have this conversation," Ben said quietly.

"No." Sierra directed her comment to Ben in an equally soft voice. "The best time would have been last night when you were trying to pull one over on me."

"That's not what I did," Ben protested.

Ryan looked from Sierra to Ben, a puzzled expression on his face, then placed a hand at the small of Sierra's back. She wondered if he could feel her shaking.

"Ben's right," Ryan said. "We should take this to my office."

Sierra pivoted and led the way, determinedly keeping her head high and her chin up, the pleasure leaking out of a morning that had started with such promise.

This was exactly why she took so few chances.

The ones she did take tended to backfire.

THE WHITMORE SIBLINGS regarded Ben with widely different expressions after the three of them retreated to a generic room at the end of a long hall. Curiosity emanated from Ryan while Sierra's lips had flatlined and her eyes had gone steely. Her brother leaned against the edge of a sleek, black desk, his legs crossed at the ankles. Sierra remained standing.

"Now tell us what this is all about," she demanded. The hair she'd worn long and loose the night before was tied back from her face. A shapeless white lab coat covered her clothes. It was as though the soft, vulnerable woman he'd kissed had never existed.

He blamed himself for that.

He'd gone about the early part of his investigation all wrong, rushing off to Indigo Springs before conducting any of the background work that was usually the foundation of his reporting.

"Yesterday morning I received an e-mail suggesting your father might know something about the death of Allison Blaine," he said.

"Allison Blaine," Ryan repeated, then shook his head. "The name doesn't ring a bell."

"She died quite a while ago." Ben struggled to keep his voice free of the emotion that threatened to clog his throat. "In a fall from a cliff."

"I remember something like that." Sierra's brows drew together. "She was a tourist, right? It seems like the town organized a search. Didn't a fisherman find her body?"

"That's about the extent of it," Ben said.

"But wasn't that, like, twenty years ago?" Sierra asked.

The date of the day that had forever altered his life was carved into Ben's mind like an engraving. The anniversary of his mother's death would be in three months. "Nineteen."

"I don't understand." Sierra shook her head. "Why are you looking into this now, after all this time? And what does our father have to do with it?"

Ben moistened his lips. "I already told you about the e-mail."

"You haven't told us what was in it," Ryan pointed out.

Do you know what really happened to your mother?

Ben didn't repeat the question aloud. His personal involvement had already clouded his usually clear judgment. If he could treat this like any other story, he'd have a much better chance of uncovering the truth. That meant not telling the Whitmores or anyone else in town he was Allison Blaine's son.

"The e-mail asked why Dr. Ryan Whitmore wasn't questioned about her death." He relayed the substance of the message, substituting "questioned" for "investigated."

"What!" Sierra cried. "Why would he be? Wasn't her death an accident?"

"It was ruled an accident," Ben clarified. "The e-mail casts doubt on that."

"Who sent this e-mail?" Sierra asked sharply.

"I don't know yet. The only fact I have is that it originated from Indigo Springs." Ben explained how the newspaper's IT department had tracked the e-mail to one of the public-access computers at the library.

"Let me get this straight," Sierra said tightly, her posture as rigid as her words. She moved closer to her silent brother, as though to demonstrate they were a united front. "You came here today to accuse our father of God only knows what because of some anonymous e-mail."

"I'm following a lead," he said. "I'm not accusing your father of anything."

"Before you cast stones, you should know he was a very good man with a spotless reputation." Color infused Sierra's cheeks even though she didn't raise her voice. "You know the festival the town is holding next weekend? He'll be honored for his civic work. The town is renaming the park Whitmore Memorial Park."

Yet another fact Ben had failed to discover before rushing to Indigo Springs.

"Why are you doing this story at all?" Ryan broke his silence, his tone far less volatile than his sister's. "Why would a Pittsburgh newspaper be interested in something that happened in Indigo Springs almost twenty years ago?"

"Allison Blaine was from Pittsburgh." Ben ignored the second, more piercing question. "Look. I didn't come here to upset anyone. Like I said, I'm exploring a tip. It's probable your father knew her. Maybe she was one of his patients."

"That's unlikely," Sierra said. "She didn't live here."

"It's still possible. She could have needed a doctor while she was in town," Ben said. "There's one way to find out. You could check your records."

"Why would we do that?" Sierra asked. "What possible benefit could it have for us?"

"It could show Mr. Nash here he's barking up the wrong tree." Ryan directed his comment to his sister. He straightened from the desk, laying a hand on her arm. He switched his attention to Ben. "Our records weren't computerized twenty years ago, but it'll only take a minute to look through our hard files and tell you if Allison Blaine was ever a patient."

Ben had been a reporter long enough not to blindly believe the Whitmores would freely share information that didn't clear their father of suspicion.

"Mind if I come along?" Ben asked in as offhand a manner as he could muster. Sierra seemed about to protest, so he added, "There are a number of ways to spell Blaine."

"I don't mind at all." Ryan let his sister precede him out the door. They followed her down the narrow hall, with Ryan talking as they went. "I need you to understand we can only confirm whether she was a patient. Even the dead are protected by doctor/patient privilege."

The narrow hall led to a small room with banks of file cabinets lining one wall. Ryan went directly to the first file cabinet and carefully flipped through the manila folders, then shrugged. "Nope. No Allison Blaine."

Ben wasn't ready to give up. "She was visiting her parents so it's possible she came into the office with one of them. Their names were Barbara and Leonard Blaine."

Ryan turned back to the files. "I don't see their files, either. Did they live in town long?"

"Not even six months, I think," Ben said.

"Must have been a healthy six months," Ryan quipped.

Even if it meant revealing his relationship to Allison Blaine, Ben couldn't ignore the third possibility. His mother could have brought one of his brothers to see a doctor.

"Is this where you keep the records for pediatric patients?" Ben asked, preparing to request the files be searched for the last name Nash.

"All those records are computerized," Ryan answered. "We became a family practice when Sierra started working here two years ago. She and I are family physicians. Our father was an internist who treated patients eighteen and over."

"Allison Blaine wasn't treated here." Sierra didn't seem the least bit curious as to why he'd asked about pediatric patients. "Your lead is a dead end."

"Not necessarily," Ben said slowly. "He might have known her personally."

"There's no way to confirm that." Ryan shut the file cabinet, almost as a signal that to the Whitmore siblings the case was closed.

"There could be." Ben was trained to recognize other avenues that might yield results. "Your mother might know whether your father was acquainted with Allison Blaine. Is she alive?"

"Alive and well," Ryan said.

"Mind telling me how I can get in touch with her?"

"Yes," Sierra retorted sharply.

At the same time, her brother answered, "She moved into a retirement community after Dad died."

"What's the name of the place?" Ben asked.

"Hold on," Sierra said before Ryan could supply the information. She moved closer to her brother so their shoulders were almost touching. "I don't think we should tell him, Ryan."

"If you don't, I'll find out from somebody else." That was the absolute truth. A good reporter could always locate somebody who was eager to talk, no matter what the subject. "Why not tell me? What are you afraid of?"

Sierra stiffened. "I'm afraid you'll upset her."

"Then come with me," he offered.

"Excuse me?"

"If you're along," Ben said, "you can make sure I'm on my best behavior."

Ben would also increase his chances of getting Sierra to listen to the apology he'd been forming since her attitude toward him had gone from hot to cold.

"What do you say?" He recognized that she'd seen the wisdom in his reply and pressed his advantage. "When you finish up here, will you take me to her?"

She chewed on her lower lip, then glanced at her brother, who gave an almost imperceptible nod. Her eyes once again fastened on Ben.

"I'll meet you in the office around two," she said.

MISSING TOURIST FOUND DEAD.

Sierra edged forward in the stiff-backed chair, getting closer to the grainy type displayed on the screen of the microfiche machine in the back corner of the public library. The smell of new carpeting mingled with the slightly musty smell of the old books shelved in the nearby reference section.

She'd come straight from her last patient of the day, determined to equip herself with as much information as possible about Allison Blaine before setting off for her mother's retirement community with Ben Nash.

She read on.

A local businessman found the body of missing tourist Allison Blaine on the banks of the Lehigh River during the early-morning hours yesterday.

Frank Sublinski, the owner of Indigo River Rafters, had hiked downriver to try out a new fly-fishing spot when he stumbled across the body sprawled amid the rocks at the edge of the river.

Police Chief Alex Rawlings said Blaine did not appear to have drowned and that her injuries were consistent with a fall. "It's pretty obvious she got too close to the edge and took a tumble," Rawlings said.

The Riverview Overlook, which provides scenic views of the Lehigh River, is located on a cliff above the section of the river where the tourist's body was discovered. Local residents have complained in recent months about the lack of a guide rail at the site, especially after the heavy spring rains eroded part of the cliff.

Blaine, a thirty-year-old Pittsburgh resident, had been visiting her parents since last week. Leonard and Barbara Blaine reported their daughter missing twenty-four hours before her body was discovered, spawning a massive search.

A camera was found near Blaine's body. Rawlings said foul play is not suspected.

Sierra hadn't remembered that Annie's father had been the one to find the tourist's body, but the rest of the article contained no surprises.

"Open and shut," Sierra whispered aloud. It was easy to imagine Allison Blaine losing her footing on the eroded cliff and falling as she pointed her camera. "So what is Ben Nash doing here?"

She hadn't found a story leading up to the incident, probably because the *Indigo Springs Gazette* was a weekly newspaper that went to press on Thursdays. By the time the paper could report that Allison Blaine was missing, her body would have been found.

She quickly scrolled through the rest of the roll of microfilm, locating only a brief item about the bouquets of flowers people had left in memoriam at the overlook. The article mentioned that Allison Blaine's parents had recently moved to town. She already knew from Ben that they hadn't stayed long.

Sierra pressed the print button on the machine, then hit Rewind. She was due to meet Ben in ten minutes. If she didn't hurry, she wouldn't put it past him to leave without her. After placing the microfilm back in the plastic container, she headed to the research desk.

The young female librarian who'd helped her access the back issues of the *Gazette* was gone, replaced by an Indigo Springs institution. Louise Wiesneski had once directed Sierra to source material for her high school research papers. More recently, the librarian checked out books Sierra used to fuel her reading habit.

"What brings you here today?" Mrs. Wiesneski asked in an authoritative voice that had the unfortunate tendency to carry. A large woman, she even looked tall sitting down. "The latest mystery? Or one of those sports biographies you're always reading?"

"Nothing that exciting." Sierra set the microfilm on the counter and devised a noncommittal answer that would satisfy the nosy librarian. "I was just using the microfiche machine."

Mrs. Wiesneski picked up the container and checked the label. "Hmm. Nobody's looked at a back issue of the *Gazette* in months, yet you're the second person today who requested this same roll of film."

"This other person," Sierra asked. "Was his name Ben Nash?"

"It most certainly was. Said he was a reporter for some newspaper in Pittsburgh. Do you know him?"

"Sort of," Sierra said absently while she prepared to go against her instincts. The other times she'd been in the library, she'd kept her conversations with Mrs. Wiesneski brief to avoid gossiping. "Did he ask you any questions?"

"As a matter of fact, he did." Mrs. Wiesneski lowered her too-loud voice, eager to share her information. "He wanted to know if I had a record of everyone who signed on to the Internet Friday morning. Well, you know how busy we get in here come tourist season. People are waiting to use the computers when we open at nine. Even if we did keep a record, which we don't, I wouldn't have told him, being as that's privileged information."

So Ben had been unsuccessful in tracking down the sender of the anonymous e-mail. Interesting but not unexpected.

"He also asked if I remembered anything about some tourist who died in Indigo Springs a long time ago," Mrs. Wiesneski continued. "Now you know me, I remember everything. Except that was before my time."

Sierra's brows must have lifted, because the other

woman kept talking. "I know sometimes it seems like I've been here forever, but it's only been seventeen years. Now are you gonna tell me what this is all about?"

Not likely, Sierra thought.

"Curiosity," Sierra said. "He asked my brother and me the same kinds of questions."

The librarian nodded, but the speculative gleam in her eyes suggested she realized Sierra had dodged the question. Her attention wavered, and she nodded to a spot behind Sierra.

"Speak of the devil," she said.

Sierra quickly turned around to see Ben Nash striding through the library straight toward them with his long, measured gait. Self-assurance poured off him, but she had the impression he'd be surprised if he knew he'd drawn every eye in the place.

"Please thank Betty for her help," Sierra said hurriedly, referring to the other librarian by name, before quickly moving away from the desk.

Whatever Ben had to say to her would be said in private.

CHAPTER FOUR

BEN WATCHED Sierra Whitmore hurry past the shelf containing the new releases with her chin high and her steps clipped, her pretty mouth turned down at the corners.

He hadn't expected her to be happy he'd tracked her down yet couldn't help wishing for the warm smile she'd greeted him with earlier. Before she'd found out who he was and why he was in town.

"Ready to go?" he asked.

"I thought we were meeting at my office."

"I took a chance you'd be here instead."

Her gaze slid to the reference desk, probably to check if the microfilm she'd been viewing was still visible. Even if he hadn't caught a glimpse of the canister, he could have easily figured out she'd come to the library to go through back issues of the *Gazette*. He'd done the same earlier that morning in his quest to find information both about the case and her father.

Her chin lifted even higher when she regarded him again. She'd shed the traditional doctor's white coat, revealing a red top that added vibrancy to her complexion and a skirt that showed off a pair of long, beautiful legs. She was undeniably attractive, but it was her underlying spunk that drew him to her, hinting at facets of her he'd yet to discover.

"There's something you should know about me," she said with spirit. "I never enter any situation unprepared. I like to know what I'm up against."

"Totally understandable," Ben said. "I can give you the phone number of the *Tribune* and the name of my managing editor if you like."

From the slight widening of her eyes, he surmised she'd thought to check out his story of what had happened to Allison Blaine, but it hadn't occurred to her to verify his credentials.

"I can find the phone number myself, thank you very much," she said.

Even on guard and distrusting, she was polite. Yet he was more interested in what was under the stuffy facade. He'd love to get another glimpse of the woman he'd kissed the night before. That wasn't going to happen unless he could make amends.

"I'm sorry about last night," he began.

She put a finger to her lips and cut her eyes at the exit. The library was fairly busy, with a few of the people perusing the bestsellers regarding them with open curiosity. Sierra led the way outside into the April sunshine.

"I'd rather the entire town didn't know what you're doing here." She spoke in the same soft voice she'd used inside the charming brick building even though the library sat atop a small hill a fair distance from the street.

"I'm not planning to keep it a secret."

"You kept it from me last night," she retorted.

"That's why I was apologizing." He scratched the back of his neck when she didn't respond, wondering what he could say to get her to understand. "In my defense, I didn't know who you were when we made plans to get together."

"Oh, really?" Disbelief dripped from her voice.

"Really. It was only when the bartender mentioned you were a doctor that I put it together."

"Is that when you decided to pull one over on me?"

"If that's what I was trying to do, why didn't I grill you about your father?"

The steel in her expression didn't melt, not even a little. "That's no excuse for not telling me you were a reporter."

He remembered how crestfallen she'd looked when her ex-boyfriend had entered the bar, prompting him to temporarily put aside his investigation. "I didn't think it was the right time to tell you."

"You thought wrong," she said.

She turned from him and walked away from the library, toward the sidewalk that cut a swath through the mix of delightful old buildings and new storefronts that made up downtown Indigo Springs. Some of the trees had started to blossom, giving the air a floral scent. He fell into step beside her.

"There are a few things you need to know before we go see my mother," she announced without looking at him.

"Shoot," he said.

"My parents grew up next door to each other. They

were married for thirty-five years. My mother was dev-astated when my father died. She says she can't re-member a time she didn't love him."

She fell silent as they maneuvered around a man in khaki shorts and hiking shoes taking a photo of a woman in front of a pretty stone building. When they were free of the pair, she pointed across the street to a lush green space shaded with tall trees. It boasted park benches, a children's play area with wooden structures and an amphitheater set well back from the road.

"That park is the one the town's renaming for my father," she said. "My mother's very proud he'll be honored in that way. The whole family is."

Ben had a better grasp of why the town was honoring Dr. Whitmore since going through recent issues of the *Indigo Springs Gazette* at the library. He'd found an article about the upcoming memorial that detailed the late doctor's involvement in a staggering number of charitable causes and civic organizations.

"I'm not trying to take anything away from your father's memory," he said gently. "I just want to figure out why somebody sent me that e-mail."

She angled her head and the sunlight caught the highlights in her brown hair. He glimpsed the warmth beneath her cool exterior and wished he could turn back the clock to last night. He considered apologiz-ing again, but didn't see how it would do any good.

"Did you consider that whoever sent the e-mail had something against my father?" she asked in a clipped voice.

"Did your father have enemies?"

"Of course not." Her response was too quick, immediately making him suspect she was hiding something. Calling her on it wouldn't be wise, especially when he could find out who had disliked Dr. Whitmore in other ways.

He took the conversation in a different direction. "It sounds like your parents were well-established in town."

"They were," she agreed.

"Then why did your mother move away?"

"She said the big house felt empty without my father," she said. "Some of her friends already lived at the retirement community and convinced her to give it a try. It's close enough she can come to town whenever she likes."

They were almost to the curb in front of Whitmore Family Practice, where he'd parked his car. "How long will it take us to drive there?"

"Forty minutes, give or take."

"Your car or mine?"

"Both." She answered so quickly she must have already decided upon the driving arrangements. "I live in the next block, as you already know. My car is the gold Lexus. You can follow me."

She never stopped walking as she delivered the news, conveying her decision wasn't open for discussion. She'd been just as clear about her refusal to accept his apology.

He swallowed his disappointment, rationalizing it was a good thing she was unwilling to explore their mutual attraction.

He'd come to Indigo Springs to unlock the mystery

of his mother's death. He couldn't let anyone, especially someone with the last name of Whitmore, distract him from his goal.

ROSEMARY WHITMORE straightened the pitcher of lemonade she'd set on the wicker table, sending the ice cubes clanking. She surveyed the tableau, then rearranged the tall glasses so they were equidistant from the pitcher.

Once she was satisfied, she sat down on one of the chairs overlooking the third fairway of Mountain Village Estates' eighteen-hole golf course. The community had been built with luxury in mind, from the well-appointed condos to amenities such as a health spa, tennis courts and swimming pool. Most days, she scheduled something to do, finding activity preferable to being alone with her thoughts.

Today, however, she needed to think. To keep her wits about her. Within moments, she sprang back up again. Cookies. She could set out a plate of cookies.

She took a pretty patterned dessert plate from a kitchen cabinet and positioned store-bought chocolate-chip cookies in an artful circle before heading back to the sunroom.

"There," she said aloud when the plate of cookies was adjacent to the lemonade. "Now I'm ready."

Except she'd never be completely prepared to face the reporter who was coming to ask about that poor woman who'd died at the Riverview Overlook.

When Sierra called to tell her about him, she'd needed to sit down to steady herself. In the first few years after it happened, she expected someone to show up at the door of the house she'd shared with Ryan. The feeling of inevitability had gradually faded until she'd almost convinced herself she was paranoid.

She couldn't fathom why, after nineteen years had passed, someone was coming calling now.

A piercing noise cut through the quiet of the place, making her jump. The doorbell. She heard the sound of the door opening, then Sierra's voice. "Hello? Mother? We're here."

Mentally scolding herself for being silly, Rosemary filled her lungs with air and exhaled slowly. Then she went to meet her guests, patting into place the blond hair she'd had styled the afternoon before.

"Sierra, darling, it's good to see you." She greeted her daughter first, lightly embracing her and wishing they'd had a moment alone. She'd heard just this morning after church that Sierra—her Sierra!—had been kissing a mystery man in front of the Blue Haven Pub. Rosemary hoped that meant she'd finally gotten over Chad Armstrong breaking up with her, although Rosemary could understand why Sierra had been heartbroken. Both Rosemary and Ryan had thought Chad was perfect for her.

"Mother, I'd like you to meet Ben Nash," Sierra said when she stepped back from the embrace. "He's the *Pittsburgh Tribune* reporter. Ben, this is my mother, Rosemary Whitmore."

She'd expected somebody unpleasant with intense, beady eyes, possibly wearing a trench coat and carrying a tape recorder. Ben Nash had none of those things. Tall and lean with a trace of a beard shadowing his strong, handsome face, Ben reminded her of her husband on those weekend mornings before he shaved. Ben's hair was even the same shade of dark brown as her husband's had been before he grayed. She blinked before she could tear up, reminding herself it was essential she keep up her guard.

"It's nice to meet you, Mrs. Whitmore." Ben stuck out his right hand and gripped hers with just the right amount of firmness.

"Oh, please call me Rosemary." She gestured behind her to the rear of the condo when they were through shaking hands. "Why don't you come with me to the sunroom."

They reached the patio in moments, emphasizing how small the condo was in relation to the large house in Indigo Springs she'd vacated after Ryan died. Memories were funny things. They'd chased her from the house where she'd been so happy, yet she hadn't been able to outrun them.

She busied herself pouring lemonade from the pitcher. On the fairway, a golfer swung at a ball and hit nothing but air. She prayed she wouldn't make a similar gaffe with Ben Nash.

When she was through handing out drinks, she sat in one of the wicker chairs that flanked the table. "Sierra tells me you wanted to ask about my husband."

"That's true." Ben sat his lemonade down and scooted forward in his chair. "Specifically in relation to a woman named Allison Blaine."

"Oh, yes. Sierra reminded me she was that unfortunate tourist who fell from the Riverview Overlook." As though Rosemary could ever forget. "A dreadful tragedy, that was."

"You remember her then?" he asked, a note of eagerness in his voice.

"Not her in particular." Careful, she warned herself. "I remembered hearing about her going missing."

"Hearing about?" He'd picked up on the pertinent words in her statement, just like she'd intended.

"We were out of town at the time." She began repeating the story she'd rehearsed. "If I'm remembering correctly, and I think I am, she died early in July. When our children were young, we went to the Jersey shore the first week of July every year. Isn't that right, Sierra?"

Her daughter nodded. "That's right."

Sierra was holding herself even more stiffly than usual, almost as though she was afraid a part of her might brush against Ben Nash if she moved. Rosemary couldn't afford to speculate on their relationship. She needed to keep her wits about her.

"Do you know if your husband was acquainted with Allison Blaine?" Ben asked.

"I don't see how he could have been." Rosemary made her eyes wide and innocent. "I already said we were on vacation when she died."

"She'd been in town for a week or two before then. Maybe he ran into her before you went on vacation." Ben reached into his back pocket and pulled something out. "Would you look at this photo and tell me if she's familiar to you?"

Rosemary took the photo. Sadness swept over her at the sight of the pretty, brown-haired woman. "Of course she looks familiar."

Ben seemed to be holding his breath.

"I remember seeing her photo in the *Gazette*." Rosemary handed the photo back to him.

Ben exhaled and frowned. "I was at the library this morning going through back issues and didn't run across her picture."

"Are you sure?" Rosemary felt her smile waver. She'd been positive the weekly newspaper had run Allison Blaine's photo.

"Very sure."

"Well, there must be an explanation." She smiled when she thought of one. "Oh, I know. There were flyers all over town when she was missing."

"I thought you said you weren't in town when she died."

Ben Nash was sharp, yet she could be smarter. "We weren't. Some of the flyers must have still been up when we returned." She didn't let her smile falter. "Can I ask what this is about?"

"I told you on the phone, Mother," Sierra interrupted. "He's an investigative reporter, talking to anyone who might have known her."

Rosemary took a dainty sip of lemonade, grateful for the cool slide of the liquid down her dry throat. Sierra had explained very little, certainly not why Ben Nash had decided to look into this particular story. Rosemary wasn't about to ask and risk coming across as too curious. She composed a noninflammatory question.

"Why did you even think she might have known my husband, Ben?"

He glanced at Sierra and a meaningful look passed between them. What was that about? Rosemary wondered. "I'm thorough."

"He knows what a good man Daddy was," Sierra blurted. Again her daughter and Ben Nash seemed to communicate without words. Rosemary almost gasped. Was this reporter the man Sierra had been kissing? Was she involved with him? As much as she wanted her daughter to move on with her life, that would not be good. "I told him about the park that's going to be renamed for him."

"A wonderful thing, isn't it?" Rosemary said. "And so well-deserved. Ryan was such a fine man, tirelessly working for the good of the community."

Even though she spoke the truth, she was possibly laying it on too thick. She stopped talking.

"Let me ask you one more question, Mrs. Whitmore," Ben said. "Is it possible your husband knew Ms. Blaine without you being aware of it?"

"No, it's not." Rosemary was well versed about anything and everything that had concerned her late husband. They hadn't kept secrets from each other. "Now is there anything else I can get you? Some cheese and crackers, perhaps?"

Ryan hesitated. "No, thank you."

She knew perfectly well all he wanted was information that could conceivably ruin her husband's good name, which was all she had left of him.

He wouldn't get it from her.

SIERRA FOLLOWED the mountain road as it lost elevation, carefully maintaining the speed of her Lexus so she didn't catch up to the convertible in front of her. The car was a metallic silver Chrysler Sebring, sleek but not flashy.

The occasional glimpse of the Sebring's bumper disappearing around one of the frequent curves verified she hadn't lost him, not that there was much danger of that. The single-lane road through the canopy of trees didn't afford Ben Nash many places to turn off.

She'd been following him since they'd left her mother's home and he'd done the unexpected, taking a turn that led away from his downtown hotel.

Her mother's assertion that her father hadn't known Allison Blaine should have signaled an end to Ben Nash's investigation, but Sierra wasn't taking anything for granted. If following him was the only way to find out if he meant to leave town or continue nosing around, so be it.

She maneuvered her Lexus through a hairpin curve before the road abruptly straightened, leading downhill to a four-way stop. Beyond the intersection was a bridge that spanned an offshoot of the Lehigh River. Ben Nash's convertible idled at the stop sign.

"Shoot," she said aloud, easing her foot off the gas. No vehicles were on the road between them. If he looked in his rearview mirror, he couldn't miss her.

The intersecting road was clear of traffic, yet his car didn't budge. Sierra slowed her Lexus to a crawl. It moved inexorably forward, gaining ground by the second, getting closer and closer to his car.

Just as she was running out of following distance,

the driver's side door of the stopped car swung open. Ben got out, then jogged toward her with athletic grace, not bothering to close the door behind him.

She looked left, then right, but all she could see were trees, empty road and the mountain laurels that seemed to be everywhere in the spring. The only way to avoid a confrontation was to swing into a U-turn and hightail it up the hill, back the way she'd come. With Ben moving toward her, though, she might run him over.

"Oh, great." She closed her eyes in mortification, opening them in time to see him standing at the window making a circular gesture.

Surrendering to the inevitable, she pressed the button that automatically rolled down the driver's side window. He braced one hand against the car and leaned down, his face filling the window opening, his eyes once again covered by dark shades.

She couldn't be sure whether the intoxicating scent she breathed was the outdoors, Ben's warm skin or a combination of the two.

"I'm headed to Indigo River Rafters to talk to Frank Sublinski," he announced.

Of course. According to the newspaper story, Annie's father had been the one who'd found Allison Blaine's body. She should have predicted his destination.

She tried to cloak her interest with a toss of her head. "What makes you think I care?"

"You've been following me for the past ten minutes."

She started to deny it, then thought what was the use.

Even James Bond would have had difficulty keeping under the radar on the Poconos's back roads.

"So?" It was the only response she could come up with under pressure.

One side of his sensuous mouth lifted. "So I'm flattered."

"Flattered?" She shook her head. "You've got it wrong. I'm not following you because I'm attracted to you."

He cocked his head, his eyebrows raising above the rim of his sunglasses. She couldn't see all of them but knew his brows were perfectly shaped, like his mouth. His lips were full for a man's, the upper one marked with a sensuous bow.

"You're not?" he asked. "I seem to remember you bringing up mutual attraction. Something about trying to get me to ask you back to my room. Am I wrong?"

"No." She winced at her honesty, her eyes shifting away from him. "I mean, yes."

"You're a terrible liar." His voice was low, similar to the purr of her idling car engine.

She inhaled and made herself look at him. A mistake. With his eyes covered by those damnable shades, her gaze fastened on his lips, reminding her of their kiss. It had been one hell of a kiss. She cleared her throat. "Despite this fantasy you've concocted, I was following you to find out what you're up to."

"You could have asked."

She watched his lips move, then jerked her gaze back up to his sunglasses.

"There aren't many things I'd refuse to do if you asked," he added in that same low, sexy voice.

Heat started low in her belly and spread. She lifted her chin, desperate to douse it for her self-preservation.

"If you get to the river before me, wait to talk to Frank Sublinski until I get there." Her voice sounded artificially loud and stilted, but that was better than shaky and aroused.

They were at a stop sign with the sun shining down on them, for goodness' sake.

"Done." He smiled, tapped the top of the rolled-down window and sauntered back to his car. He was tall and broad-shouldered, his rear end among the finest she'd ever seen.

She groaned.

In college she'd had boy-crazy friends who were always talking about pheromones and instant attraction, which she'd never experienced herself.

Until now.

Why did it have to be with Ben Nash?

POLKA MUSIC FILLED the warehouse-type building that housed Indigo River Rafters, causing Ben to reassess his opinion of Frank Sublinski before they'd even met.

He would have expected a man who'd spent most of his life outdoors to be listening to country music.

The last tour group must have already come off the river and gone, because he and Sierra were the only ones in the shop. If not for the unlocked door and the lively beat of the polka, the business would have seemed closed.

"Interesting choice of music," Ben remarked to Sierra.

She stood half a body length away, nearer the shelf of suntan lotions than him. Since their arrival, she'd been careful to keep at least that much distance between them at all times.

"Mr. Sublinski's from Poland," she said. "He visited his family last summer. Since then, Annie says he plays polkas all the time."

That was the first thing she'd said to him since they'd arrived. He thought about casually moving closer, but didn't want to crowd her, not after her inadvertent admission there was something between them. He couldn't say for certain what he wanted of her except her good opinion. He wouldn't get that by forcing her to acknowledge truths she wasn't ready to face.

"He probably misses his family." Ben knew what that was like, except in his case there'd been no remedy for missing his mother. The only place he could visit her was the graveyard.

"I don't know what you hope to accomplish by talking to him," Sierra said, edging even farther from him.

"What any reporter hopes for," Ben said. "The truth."

"My mother told you the truth. My father didn't know Allison Blaine."

Ben didn't have any strong cause to doubt Rosemary Whitmore aside from a healthy skepticism she was aware of everything that had gone on in her husband's life. Telling Sierra that wouldn't serve any purpose.

"Then my motive's the same as it's always been. I'm trying to get to the truth of why someone sent me that e-mail," he said.

"Hello? Somebody there?" A gray-haired man with a wiry build and deeply tanned skin appeared from the back of the shop, speaking loudly to be heard above the music. His face relaxed into a smile. "Oh, hey, Sierra. What brings you out here?"

When she started to answer, he put up his index finger. "Wait 'til I turn off my polkas. See this CD player? Annie gave it to me for my birthday. Best present I ever got."

He pressed a button on the player and the shop abruptly went silent. Not for long. Frank Sublinski wasn't a large man, but he had an infectious energy that filled up a room.

"I haven't seen you since Annie's wedding and that was back in February." He kept his focus on Sierra as he moved toward them, traveling with a slight limp. "How have you been?"

"I'm fine, Mr. Sublinski," Sierra said politely. "How about you?"

"Can't complain 'cept I dropped a kayak on my foot today. Hurts like the dickens. And how many times do I have to tell you to call me Frank?" He shook his gray head. "Everybody else does, and we're practically family."

"Yes, sir."

"Frank. Not 'sir.'" He indicated Ben with a nod of his head. "Who's this you've got with you? Your new boyfriend?"

"He's not my boyfriend." Sierra sounded authoritative, but her cheeks were turning pink. "I don't have a new boyfriend."

"I thought Annie said…" The shop owner's voice trailed off and he stuck out a hand to Ben. "Never mind. I'm Frank Sublinski. And you are?"

Ben told him, providing as many details as possible without mentioning Sierra's late father.

Frank leaned with his back against the counter, keeping his weight off his sore foot. "Yeah, I found her. A sad business that was. I'm kind of isolated here. Didn't know the whole town was looking for her. I woke up early to get in some fishing before I opened up shop and hiked downriver to one of my favorite spots. And there she was."

Frank's expression tightened at the memory. Ben tried to blot out his mental image of what the older man must have seen. His palms stung, making him realize his short nails dug into the skin as he clenched his hands into fists. He relaxed his fingers.

"Could you tell what had happened to her?" Ben asked.

"She fell from the overlook. That was pretty clear from where I found her," Frank said. "The police chief agreed with me."

"Alex Rawlings?"

"How did you know I was talking about Alex?" Frank asked. "Alex retired…must have been ten years ago."

"I read the *Indigo Springs Gazette* story," Ben said.

"Then you already know as much as I can tell you," Frank said.

"I read the story, too," Sierra said. "The newspaper implied she was taking photos and lost her balance."

Frank straightened from the counter. "That's not the way it was. It's been so long I forgot about the newspaper reporter getting the part about the camera wrong."

Ben tensed. "Wrong how?"

Earlier yesterday at the library wasn't the first time Ben had read the newspaper account of his mother's death. Years ago, before his father had moved across the state from Pittsburgh to start a life with another woman, Ben had discovered a yellowed copy of the article hidden inside a hardback copy of *To Kill a Mockingbird*. He'd picked up the book to read because it had been his mother's favorite.

"The camera wasn't hers," Frank said. "It was mine. I took it along that morning to get a shot of the sunset. Must have dropped it when I found her."

Ben took a step backward, staggered by Frank's assertion. He'd always believed his mother had gone to the overlook to photograph the scenery yet now realized his sole source of information in that regard was the *Indigo Springs Gazette*.

Things that had never quite made sense seemed even more suspicious now. His mother had disappeared at dusk, which he supposed could have yielded some interesting images for a photographer who knew what she was doing. If that wasn't the case, why had she been at the overlook in the gathering gloom? Had she been meeting somebody?

"Had you ever seen Allison Blaine before that morning?" Ben asked.

"Nope," Frank said.

"Did you remember hearing anything about her? Like, for example, if she'd become friends with any of the town residents?" Ben avoided looking at Sierra when he asked the question, although he could sense her disapproval.

"Can't say that I did." Frank shook his head while his eyes narrowed. "Why? Are you thinking she wasn't alone at that overlook when she fell?"

"Anything's possible." His peripheral vision picked up Sierra stiffening in disapproval.

"Then why wasn't there more of an investigation?" Frank asked.

Why wasn't Dr. Ryan Whitmore ever investigated?

"That's what I'm trying to find out," Ben replied.

"Far be it from me to tell a big-city reporter how to do his job," Frank said, "but it seems to me you're chasing shadows."

With Ben's supply of questions exhausted, they left the shop a short time later. The trees that grew near the flowing river cast shadows over the grassy parking lot. It was dusk, the time of day his mother had died.

"Why didn't you just ask him if he'd heard any rumors linking my father to Allison Blaine?" Sierra walked quickly toward the spot where they'd parked their cars side by side, her steps seeming as angry as her words. "It's what you wanted to know, isn't it?"

"I didn't want to put words in his mouth."

"Yet you had no trouble letting an anonymous e-mail put thoughts in your head."

"I haven't reached any conclusions yet," Ben denied. "I'm keeping my mind open."

She glared up at him. "Is it open to the ulterior motive of the person who sent you that e-mail?"

"I'll know the answer to that question once I figure out who sent it." He stopped beside her car and decided to go for broke. "I got the impression earlier you might have a guess as to who that might be. Want to share it with me?"

"You're wrong," she said, her eyes darting away from his. "I don't have a clue."

She was lying. He knew that as clearly as what her answer would be if he asked her to dinner. He asked anyway.

"Would you like to go out with me tonight?"

"You're unbelievable." She got in her car and banged the door shut. She started the ignition, slammed the gearshift into Drive and gunned the engine so abruptly the tires kicked up dirt and grass as she pulled away.

He sighed. He couldn't blame her for believing his motive for seeking her company was to learn more about her father.

It would be much, much simpler if that were the only reason.

CHAPTER FIVE

THE INTERIOR OF Quincy Coleman's house was nothing like Sierra had imagined. Terra-cotta tile and creamy walls provided a backdrop for overstuffed furniture covered in fabrics of rusts, tans and browns.

The overall effect was casual and soothing instead of elegant and unapproachable, which was how Sierra had always thought of the Coleman residence—and the man who lived there.

"I knew Annie was getting somebody to fill in for her on the committee, but nobody told me it was you," Quincy said after he'd ushered her inside early Sunday afternoon.

A small, trim man in his sixties who'd been president of the local bank before he retired, Coleman was dressed in khaki slacks, loafers and a long-sleeved, button-down shirt open at the collar. It wasn't exactly casual wear, but Sierra couldn't remember the man who'd despised her father wearing anything other than a suit.

At that moment, she almost hated Ben Nash. If he hadn't come to town with his incessant questions, she wouldn't feel compelled to do some detective work to determine if Coleman had sent the e-mail that had brought the media to Indigo Springs.

She wondered where Ben was right now and why she hadn't seen him snooping around that morning. She'd had breakfast a second time at Jimmy's Diner, this time sitting at the counter, before attending church. Both were logical places for him to show up.

She thrust Ben Nash out of her mind and focused on Coleman.

"I didn't tell Annie I could do it until this morning." Sierra kept her true motivation to herself. She fully intended to confront the unpleasant little man. But not yet. First she needed to figure out what he was up to.

"That explains it. Allow me to be the first to welcome you." Coleman smiled at her, the only time Sierra could remember that happening. It was quite a nice smile, with his eyes crinkling at the corners. "Everybody's in the family room except Charlie Bradford. Our new mayor couldn't make it. My wife's not home, but she put out quite a spread before she left. Feel free to help yourself."

Quincy had reconciled with his wife last summer after he'd disappeared and Mrs. Coleman had been part of a frantic search to find him. Most people in town had suspected foul play, but it turned out Quincy had been stranded after having fallen off a motorbike and broken his leg.

It seemed ironic that she was in Coleman's house because of another person who'd turned up missing in Indigo Springs. Allison Blaine hadn't been as lucky as Quincy, but Sierra seriously doubted her death had been anything other than accidental. No matter what Ben Nash's presence in town implied.

"Let's have a round of applause, everyone. More help has arrived," Coleman announced in a loud, cheerful voice when they reached his family room.

The four people already in the room clapped. A curly-haired woman Sierra recognized as the receptionist at Sara Brenneman's law firm placed her fingers at either side of her mouth and whistled.

"Hi," the woman with the curly hair said brightly. "I'm Laurie Grieb. We went to high school together, but you probably don't remember me. I was sort of a dork back then."

Sierra couldn't recall her from high school, which seemed unforgivable. She should say something, but couldn't think what. She nodded and smiled, disappointed in herself.

There were murmurs of greetings from the others in the room. Sierra knew all of them by name. Sara sat on the sofa between Laurie Grieb and Jill Jacobi, an occasional bartender at the Blue Haven Pub who'd always had a friendly smile and some nice words since she'd moved to town not even a year ago.

The fifth member of the committee, seated in an armchair slightly apart from the group, was Chad Armstrong. He had on the same dark slacks, gray dress shirt and muted tie he'd worn to church, where she'd been careful to avoid him.

"Nice to see you here, Sierra." There was little inflection in Chad's voice, preventing Sierra from determining if he really meant it.

She prayed her throat wouldn't clog, the way it had every other time she'd seen him since the breakup.

"Hello, Chad." Thank goodness she didn't falter under his intense scrutiny, no doubt brought on by that show she and Ben Nash had put on in front of the Blue Haven.

Coleman sat down on the love seat that matched the sofa. The only empty seat in the room was next to him. Sierra poured herself a glass of iced tea and took the space beside Coleman, dismayed to discover she was directly facing Chad.

"Since Sierra's here, let's start by talking about the renaming of the park," Sara suggested. "We're having a special signpost erected. Chad suggested we include an engraved image of a man stretching out his hand in addition to information about Dr. Whitmore."

"When I think of your father, I think of a helping hand." Chad addressed his comment to Sierra. She didn't doubt its sincerity. Her father had been instrumental in getting Chad his job at the drugstore pharmacy.

"I didn't know Dr. Whitmore, but I have an idea," Jill Jacobi piped up. "If the dedication ceremony is after the parade on Sunday, we'd be guaranteed a crowd. That way, it'd be a fitting tribute."

"Excellent idea," Coleman said. "The more people who are there, the better."

Sierra turned sharply to gaze at him, expecting to find a smirk playing about his mouth. It wasn't there. "Do you mean that?"

"Of course I do." Coleman didn't seem to give the

answer any thought. He even looked and sounded sincere.

"Quincy was the one who suggested we rename the park for your father," Chad elaborated. "He said it was past time we honored him for his civic work, and we all agreed."

Sierra's mind reeled, trying to process the ramifications of the revelation as the committee moved on to potential parking problems, sponsorships and finally publicity. She barely got her composure back in time to ask when a banner advertising the festival would be stretched across Main Street.

"Would you believe we hadn't thought of that?" Coleman put a hand to his gray head. "First day on the committee and you're already contributing. We're working with Porter's Printing. I'll get right on it."

The meeting took the better part of two hours, with the group agreeing to reconvene on Thursday, the day before the festival began.

"Eat some of this food before you go," Coleman urged. "It's way too much for the wife and me."

The other committee members rose and headed to the table where the food was set out. Quincy Coleman didn't budge.

"Could I speak with you a moment, Sierra?" he asked in a soft voice before she could rise.

She didn't reply, but gave him her attention.

"Considering your father and I weren't friends, you were probably surprised it was my suggestion to honor him," he said so only she could hear. "I'm not proud of the way I treated him when he was alive. I can't make it up to him now that he's gone, but I thought this would help his memory live on."

"Then you didn't send that e-mail?"

His brow furrowed. "What e-mail?"

"The one to the newspaper reporter?"

He continued to look at her blankly. "You mean about the festival? I don't do e-mail. I call people on the phone."

"Oh. Right." She bit her lip while she regarded him, then nodded her head and rose. "Well, thank you for what you said."

She gathered her composure and crossed the room to the table of food where Sara talked with Laurie Grieb.

"Are you sure you're okay?" she overheard Sara ask Laurie as she approached.

"I'm great," Laurie announced, although she didn't look very good. Her skin was pale and the faintest trace of perspiration glistened above her upper lip. "I just need to go, is all. You know that Kenny of mine. Since we got back together, he can barely stand to be away from me."

She pivoted and started to walk almost into Sierra. "Sorry."

Laurie kept going, making a quick exit. The attorney watched her go, a concerned expression clouding her features. "You're a doctor," she said to Sierra. "Did she look okay to you?"

"It's hard to tell from a glance. Why? I heard Laurie say she was fine."

"She's just seemed…off lately." Sara waved a hand. "I'm probably worrying for nothing. So tell me, is being on the planning committee everything Annie cracked it up to be? She needed somebody to take her place so badly she said she was going to exaggerate."

"I think it'll be fun." Sierra was surprised to realize she was telling the truth. She pulled the business card for her friend's bridal boutique out of the pocket of her pants and handed it to the bride-to-be. "Before I forget, here's that information on my friend's boutique. She has a wonderful selection. I'm sure you'll find something you like."

"Cool." Sara examined the card. "Oh, great. She's open on Wednesdays until nine o'clock. Annie says I need to get a dress ASAP. If she can go to Harrisburg after she gets off the river on Wednesday, maybe you could come with us."

"Me?" Sierra pointed to her chest and felt her jaw drop. "Why would you want me to come?"

"The wedding dress you helped Annie pick out was gorgeous. She says you instantly knew what would look good and what wouldn't."

Sierra had gotten addicted to quality clothing in her teen years when she'd briefly done some modeling, but her classic fashion sense hardly matched Sara's sense of style.

"Are you sure?" She surveyed the other woman's lime-green pants and matching short-sleeved jacket, which she carried off with her trademark flair. "You don't seem to have any problem looking terrific."

"What a nice thing to say." Sara stabbed a cube of cheddar cheese with a toothpick. "But you can't talk me out of enlisting all the help I can get. This girl's only getting married once."

"If you're sure…" Sierra said.

"I'm sure. I'll get back to you with a time." The lawyer popped the piece of cheese in her mouth, chewed, swallowed, then grinned. "Thanks for letting me rope you in."

Out of the corner of her eye, Sierra noticed Chad disengaging himself from a group that now included Quincy Coleman. He was coming around the table and heading straight for her.

"I've got to be going," she told Sara.

The heels of her shoes tapped against the tile of the foyer as she hurried for the door while trying to keep up the illusion that she wasn't rushing.

"Sierra, wait!" Chad's voice trailed her.

She considered pretending she hadn't heard him, then imagined him chasing her down on the manicured front lawn. Resigned, she pasted on a smile and pivoted.

"I'm glad I caught you." He sounded slightly out of breath. "I couldn't let you leave before I told you what a welcome addition you are to the committee. You had some great suggestions."

"You sound surprised."

She knew him well enough to recognize that his sharp intake of breath and pursed lips meant she'd hit the mark. "Of course I'm not surprised."

"Then thank you." She turned from him and resumed her exit, letting herself out of the house through the mahogany door with the stained-glass insets.

Chad fell in to step beside her. It seemed appropriate the sun took that moment to duck behind a cloud.

"How are you?" He posed the question he hadn't bothered to ask in the weeks after he'd dumped her.

"Well." She kept walking.

"Anything new going on with you?"

"Why don't you just ask me about the man you saw me kissing?"

She glanced sideways and noted his eyes widened slightly.

"Okay. Who was he?"

Sierra could have screamed—at herself. Why had she invited that question? She couldn't very well inform him Ben Nash was a reporter trying to tie her father to the death of an ill-fated tourist.

She cleared her throat, desperately trying to form an answer. Her back was to the road, but she was vaguely aware of the sound of a car engine cutting through the quiet of the street.

"He's—" Sierra began.

"Sierra." A low male voice followed the sound of a car door opening.

Her head jerked up, her eyes barely able to acknowledge what her ears had already told her. The driver of the car was Ben Nash. If not for him and his questions, she would have found a way to refuse the invitation to join the festival committee. And she wouldn't be here in this uncomfortable situation with Chad Armstrong.

"Sorry I'm late." He wore jeans and a navy blue shirt open at the collar, highlighting the beginnings of his beard, yet he moved with the confidence of a freshly shaven man dressed in a tuxedo.

He planted a quick kiss on her lips, which were open and slightly agape, then stuck out a hand to Chad. "Ben Nash."

Ben's arrival had snagged Sierra as effectively as if he'd baited her with chocolate, but now she transferred her attention to Chad. His complexion grew even more ashen when he took Ben's hand.

"Chad Armstrong."

"I hate to shake your hand and run, but Sierra and I have dinner plans." Ben grabbed her hand, squeezing gently. "Ready, Sierra?"

Unable to decide whether she was being rescued or abducted, she struggled not to stammer. She wasn't sure what she was going to say until she said it. "I'm ready."

Ben tugged gently on her hand, putting distance between them and Chad.

"Good to meet you, Chad," Ben tossed over his shoulder while he clicked the remote that unlocked the passenger door of his convertible.

Sierra could either get in the car or explain her relationship with Ben to her ex-boyfriend, which was no choice at all.

BEN HADN'T EXPECTED anything about his return to Indigo Springs to be pleasant, yet couldn't suppress the smile teasing the corners of his mouth.

That was twice in three days he'd been able to help Sierra out of a jam with her ex-boyfriend.

"If I didn't know better," Sierra said after they traveled an entire block, speaking loudly so her voice wasn't swept away by the wind, "you'd have me believing we actually have a date."

"I thought you could use the moral support." He glanced away from the road at her. She held her hair in place even though the windshield blocked the worst of the breeze. She'd worn red yesterday, but today was dressed in a scoop-necked print blouse in shades of cream and brown that she paired with tan-colored linen pants. Although she looked classically beautiful, he got the impression she was hiding her true personality behind the clothes. "Your sister-in-law told me where to find you."

"Annie?" She looked positively mistrustful. "Were you bothering Ryan again?"

He laughed at her choice of verbs. "I had another question for her father, but he was guiding a trip so I bothered Annie instead."

"And she just happened to fill you in on what I was doing today?"

"That about sums it up," he said. "She was a lot more talkative when she figured out I was the guy you went out with Friday night."

Sierra covered her mouth, making him wonder exactly what had gone on between the two women before he'd met Sierra at the Blue Haven. Whatever it was, Annie had seemed delighted by it.

"She heard about the kiss, too." He might as well provide full disclosure. "You know, this town doesn't seem that small with all the tourist traffic you get. It's amazing how word gets around."

"Does she know you work for a newspaper?"

"By now, I think everybody does."

Her stomach lurched. "Does that mean she knows you're investigating my father?"

"Not unless your brother told her," Ben said. "I don't need to bring up your father's name every time I talk to somebody."

"Really? Now why don't I believe that?"

"Because you're very distrustful." He pulled the Sebring to a curb in front of what he'd heard was the best Italian restaurant in town, not that there was much competition.

"No, seriously." Now that the car wasn't moving, it sounded as though Annie had shouted the response. She lowered her voice. "Why should I believe you'd keep my father's name out of your investigation?"

"Because it's the truth."

She'd carefully avoided looking at him during the drive, but now turned to face him, her distrust evident in the depths of her green eyes. "Isn't my father the reason you're in Indigo Springs?"

"I'm here to find out what really happened to Allison Blaine," he said. "If your father knew her, his name will come up in conversation."

Her nose wrinkled. "That's not how you usually operate, is it?"

That was putting it mildly. Ben favored the direct approach, whether professionally or personally. He didn't have the time or the patience for tact when he was chasing a story.

"No," he said. "It's not."

A young couple holding hands stopped to read the

menu posted in front of Angelo's before disappearing inside. If Ben grabbed for Sierra's hand when Chad Armstrong wasn't around as a witness, she'd almost definitely snatch it back.

"Then why change now?" she asked.

He paused to consider the question. He was a skilled enough interviewer that he could find out about Dr. Whitmore in a roundabout manner, yet it would unquestionably slow down his process.

"Because you want me to," he said.

Her mouth dropped open, then closed. She blinked, as though trying to see him more clearly.

"It only seems fair, then," he continued with more confidence than he felt, "that you agree to have dinner with me."

"Yes," she said softly.

The answer made his break from protocol seem well worth the trouble. So did asking the hostess to seat them at a quiet table away from the general cacophony in the main part of the restaurant. A candle in the center of the table glowed while soft music played. The scents of garlic bread and tomato sauce enveloped them.

She sipped white wine while they waited for their entrees to be prepared. Her appearance was diametrically opposed to the woman in the tight jeans and low-cut shirt who'd ordered whiskey at the Blue Haven yet neither incarnation seemed quite right.

"I'm trying to figure out your ulterior motive for asking me to dinner," she said over the rim of her wineglass.

"What if I don't have one? What if I asked you out because I enjoy your company?"

"Am I supposed to believe that?" she asked, clearly teasing.

"That's a strange question coming from a beautiful woman."

She tensed, as though she wasn't used to compliments. His opinion of Chad Armstrong took a deeper nosedive.

"With those kind of lines," she said, "you must be quite popular with women."

He put his elbows on the table, rested his chin on his hands and smiled at her. "If that's your way of asking if I have a girlfriend, the answer's no. I'm completely available."

"That wasn't what I was doing." She twisted the stem of her wineglass between her fingers before setting down the glass.

"Why not? It's the kind of question people ask when they're on a date."

"This isn't a date," she denied.

"Sure, it is. I asked you to dinner. You said yes. That's a date in my book."

"But…" She moved her hand. It bumped her wineglass, tipping it over. Pale liquid spilled over the table.

He took his cloth napkin from his lap, then reached across the table and dabbed at the spill. A waiter quickly appeared to assist them, mopping up the rest of the wine.

"I'm so sorry," Sierra said when the crisis was over. "I don't know what got into me."

"I do," Ben said. "You got nervous when I said we were on a date. Why is that?"

"I did not," she began, then ran a hand over her hair. Even though she was wearing it up instead of in that long sexy free fall, she still looked gorgeous. "Okay, maybe I did. It's just that I haven't been on a date with anyone other than Chad in years."

"Don't tell me he was your high school boyfriend."

"Not exactly, although we did go to the senior prom together. We'd see each other in the summers when we were both home from college, but we didn't become exclusive until I finished med school."

"When you were doing your residency."

"That's right," she said. "Mine was at a hospital in Boston. Chad was finishing up his doctorate in pharmacy at Northeastern. After he graduated, Dad got him the job here in town."

"Your *father* got him his job?" he repeated.

She bit her lower lip, as though she hadn't meant to divulge that last piece of information. "Chad probably would have gotten hired on his own. My father just put a good word in for him."

Her slipup painted a more vivid picture of her relationship with her ex. The father she'd adored had been on board with her choice of men.

"It sounds like you didn't see much of Armstrong until you finished your residency and moved back home," he said.

"I guess you could say that," she said. "Except I haven't seen much of him these past few years, either."

"Why's that?"

She stared down at the table before returning her gaze to him. "My dad died a month after I started working for him."

"A heart attack, right?" He knew the cause of death from his research on the man. "How did it happen?"

She seemed to be debating with herself whether to tell him, reminding Ben she didn't trust him. He wished he could reassure her on that count, but he wasn't yet convinced her father hadn't been involved in his mother's death.

"He was home alone," she said woodenly. "By the time my mother found him, he was dead."

"No warning signs?"

"I don't know. You'd think so, with him being a physician, especially since he'd had a minor heart attack about ten years before he died." Her eyes took on a sad, faraway look. "Maybe it would have been different if it had happened in the office with people around."

"I'm sorry." He covered her hand with his, striving to convey his sincerity. From everything he'd learned so far, her father had been a saint. Even if he was the devil incarnate, Ben wouldn't wish the pain of his death on Sierra.

"Are you still swamped at work?" he asked after a moment.

"Not so much since Ryan joined the practice," she said. "I broke my leg last summer in a car accident, and he moved back to town to help me out."

He kept his hand on hers. "Was it a bad accident?"

"Bad enough. It was dark and rainy. I was going too fast, and my car skidded off a road and hit a tree. I was lucky it wasn't worse." She told the story matter-of-factly, the way she did most things. "Anyway, once I recovered, Ryan stayed on."

"And you finally had more time to spend with Armstrong," he finished, bringing their conversation full circle.

"Yes, finally." Sierra affected a little shrug. "Except you know how that worked out."

"Your relationship should have ended long before it did."

She pulled her hand from under his and gave him a chilly look. "What do you mean by that?"

"You never really knew the guy very well, did you? I mean, you couldn't invest much in a relationship when you were in residency and starting a career. You and Armstrong obviously weren't a good fit."

"I thought we were." She sounded defensive.

"I only just met the guy and I know you're not," he said. "He's way too subdued for you."

"And you know this how?"

"I'm observant." He grinned. "That's why the newspaper pays me the big bucks."

"So what have you observed about me?" She sounded skeptical, as though his assessment couldn't possibly be correct.

"You need to be around people who will bring out the extrovert in you," he announced.

She took a sip of her refilled glass of wine. "Like you?"

"You can't deny I can get your temper flaring," he said. "But not only me. You should let other people see how much fun you can be."

She laughed without humor. "Oh, come on. I told you Chad broke up with me because I'm boring."

"Armstrong's an idiot," he said. "The woman I met the other night was not boring."

"She wasn't me, either. I was trying on a new personality for size. It didn't fit."

A waiter appeared with their plates of food. Before he could set them down, Ben raised a finger. "Could you make those to go?"

The waiter paused with their plates in midair. "Um, yeah. I guess."

"What are you doing?" Sierra asked when the waiter left them to do as Ben asked.

"Proving a point," he said. "Are you game?"

She nodded, just like he knew she would.

"APRIL'S A LITTLE COOL for alfresco dining," Sierra said from the passenger seat of Ben's parked convertible. The top was down, and the temperature felt to be in the fifties.

"Let's see what I can do about that." Ben put an arm around her, gently pulling her as close as the gearshift would allow. She tensed, waiting for him to act on the sexual tension that had been simmering between them. When it became clear he didn't intend to kiss her, she relaxed. Her reward was a flash of warmth.

"Better?" he asked. "Because I'm not ready to leave."

Sierra wasn't, either. After they'd left the restaurant with their take-out food, Ben had driven the convertible to a spot along the Lehigh River not far from Indigo River Rafters.

He'd been good company, listening to her reservations about being a member of the festival committee and letting her run some ideas by him. He'd expanded on them, seconding her notion to recognize the town's military heroes and suggesting they receive free tickets to some of the paid events.

She felt herself relaxing, the responsibilities she'd agreed to take on not quite as daunting. It was too difficult to remain close to each other with the gearshift in the way. When they separated and leaned back against the headrests, however, their faces were as close together as possible.

She raised her eyes. The lights from the city were distant enough not to dilute the beauty of the night sky. Stars twinkled overhead like tiny white sequins, so numerous they lit up the blackness. It was surprisingly loud, with the voices of frogs, insects and owls mingling in song.

"What's your favorite constellation?" Ben asked.

"Pleiades. Hands down," she said immediately. "Although it's more of a star grouping than a constellation."

"Ah, the Seven Sisters," he said. "I should have figured a professional woman like you would favor the girls."

"That's not why." She lowered her voice to a whisper. "It's because of the Pleiadeans."

"Pleiadeans?"

"The humanlike extraterrestrials who originate from the stars. They live on the planet Erra. You've probably never heard of it, right? That's because Erra's located in an alternate dimension."

"What?" His face took on a comical expression of shock.

"You're right to worry." She gazed at him in all seriousness. "The Pleiadeans who've come to earth are big on warnings that humanity is heading toward self-destruction."

"Come to earth?" His face went through a workout in skepticism, and she could tell he was carefully choosing his words. "You believe there are aliens among us?"

"Oh, yes." She made her eyes wide and earnest. "And the only way to tell them apart from actual earthlings is to prick their fingers to see if their blood runs green."

His mouth dropped open.

Her lips trembled as she tried to hold back a laugh. It was no use. It tumbled forth, a burst of mirth. "Oh, that was fun. You should see your face."

"You were teasing me?"

"Not about the Pleiadean lore," she said, still chuckling. "That part's on the level and quite interesting, although I did make up the part about the green blood. I don't actually believe any of it."

"You had me going," he said.

"I didn't even get around to the Pleiadeans and the CIA mind-control conspiracies," she said.

"And Armstrong said you were boring," he remarked, shaking his head.

"I never told Chad about the Pleiadeans," she said. "He wouldn't appreciate it."

"He didn't appreciate a lot of fine things." His eyes lingered on her face.

Pleasure shot through her at his compliment, no

doubt reflected in her smile. "So what's your favorite constellation?"

"After your entertaining answer, I'm ashamed to say it's the Big Dipper," he said. "Mostly because it's the only one I can ever pick out."

"It just takes practice, is all." She leaned her head back once again and let her eyes feast. "Once you find Orion's belt, it's pretty easy to go from there."

"How come you know so much about the stars?"

"When you grow up in a small town, you find ways to amuse yourself," she said. "If I'd known we were going to stargaze, I would have dug up my binoculars."

"Why'd you become a doctor instead of an astronomer?"

"It's all I ever thought about doing," she explained.

"Because of your dad?"

"You're good at that," she said instead of answering.

"At what?"

"Asking questions," she said. "But I've answered enough of them. It's my turn. What can you tell me about your family?"

"What do you want to know?" He sounded wary.

"Where you grew up, how many sisters and brothers you have, if you're close to them."

"Pittsburgh. No sisters. Two brothers. And no, we're not close."

"That's not fair," she said when he failed to expand on his answers. "You hardly told me anything."

"Not a whole lot to tell," he said. "Things were a little…unsettled when I was growing up. Then just before I went off to college, my father got remarried and moved to Philadelphia so his new wife could be near her family. My brothers were ten and twelve at the time so it wasn't like I had a whole lot in common with them."

"They lived with your father and stepmother in Philadelphia?" She was surprised. She inferred from his comment about his "unsettled" family life that his parents were divorced. In most cases, the children of divorce stayed with their mother.

"Yeah," he said. "I went to college at Pitt, which is far enough from Philly that I didn't visit much. My apartment had a twelve-month lease so I spent summers in Pittsburgh, scrounging up whatever jobs I could."

"How about after you graduated? Is that when you started working at the *Tribune?*"

"I've only been there a few years. Before then, I got around. Erie. Altoona. Johnstown. I worked at all those newspapers." He seemed suddenly uncomfortable, as though he didn't like talking about himself. "So back to my question—did you decide to become a doctor because of your dad?"

She didn't see any harm in letting him change the subject, especially since she'd managed to find out a little more about him. "Yeah, I did. Whenever he'd talk about his day, it was just so impressive, the difference he made in peoples' lives." It suddenly seemed important he understand exactly what sort of man her father was. "He was one of those larger-than-life characters. Everybody in town liked and respected him."

"Everybody except Quincy Coleman," he said.

A shock wave traveled through her body. "What do you know about Quincy Coleman?"

"Just what I've heard around town," he said casually, "that he and your dad didn't get along."

She scooted away from him on the leather of the bucket seat. "I thought you were leaving my father's name out of your investigation."

"Not when someone else brings him up," he said. "So did you ask Quincy if he was the one who sent the e-mail?"

His motivation suddenly became stunningly, embarrassingly clear. "You came by Coleman's house to talk to him. It wasn't to give me moral support at all."

"That's not true," he said.

"You don't plan to interview him?"

"Sure I do." He ran a hand over his lower face. "A man can have more than one reason for acting, you know. I *am* here in town working on a story."

And she'd do best to remember that. She shook her head, incensed at him for duping her, but even angrier at herself for forgetting, even for a single second, that he was a journalist.

"I'll tell you what I found out, but only so you can get it through your head the type of man my father was," she said. "Even Quincy acknowledges it. He feels so badly about how he treated my father he was the one who suggested the memorial."

"Did you ask him about the e-mail?"

"I did," she said woodenly, "and he didn't know what I was talking about."

"That's good information," he said.

She'd do well to remember information was what he was after. She thought back over the last few hours, mentally tabulating how many times the conversation had swung around to her father. She felt sick to her stomach.

"You've been pumping me all night for information about my father," she accused.

"You're the one who keeps bringing him up."

"Only because you're a master manipulator," she said. "That's what reporters do, isn't it? Steer the conversation to what they want to know."

"That's not what I was doing," he said.

"So you're satisfied my father didn't know Allison Blaine?"

"No, I'm not," he said. "But one thing doesn't have anything to do with the other."

"How can you say that? This is my father we're talking about. You obviously spent some time digging up information on him. What exactly are you trying to prove?"

"I'm trying to prove Allison Blaine's death wasn't accidental."

"What?" She should have expected the answer, yet it sounded shocking when stated so boldly.

"Too many things don't add up," he said. "First the e-mail and now the camera. If she wasn't photographing anything, there was no strong reason for her to be at the lookout once darkness hit."

"She could have stopped to check if it was still light enough to see the view." The reason sounded lame even to her ears.

"Then why was she close enough to the edge to fall?"

"Are you saying somebody pushed her?" The chill of the night penetrated her light jacket. "Are you implying it was my father?"

"I'm not implying anything."

She was shaking, not from the cold, but from anger. She remembered something else he'd said earlier, something she should have questioned. "Why did you go back to see Frank Sublinski?"

"I'm having a hard time tracking down Alex Rawlings." He named the former police chief. "I thought Frank might have some idea of how to go about it. He didn't."

Sierra, on the other hand, had Alex Rawlings's contact information written down in her address book. Not that she'd share it with Ben.

"Take me home," she ordered.

He put up the convertible top and did as she asked, driving in silence until they reached the town, which was shutting down for the night. He didn't speak until he put the car in Park in front of her town house.

"I know you won't believe this, but I asked you out tonight because I wanted to be with you," he said.

"You're right. I don't believe you."

She heard his heavy exhalation of breath.

"I'd love to see you again, but I guess that's out of the question?"

"On the contrary, you'll be seeing a lot of me," she said. "I plan to keep tabs on what you're up to."

She got out of the car and slammed the door. What

did it say about her, she wondered, that even after what happened tonight she was actually looking forward to seeing him again?

CHAPTER SIX

LOUD, RELENTLESS laughter erupted, like the sound-track at a fun house. The laughter was directed at her. Sierra had no doubt of that.

Suddenly, mirrors surrounded her, all of them reflecting Ben Nash's compelling face. His mouth was open, his teeth flashing, his eyes mocking.

The sound traveled through her like barbed wire, the jagged edges cutting into her thoughts. It was no less than she deserved for falling for his act a second time.

He laughed again, loud enough that her eyes snapped open. To blackness.

She blinked, confused about why she could no longer see Ben. A bedroom slowly came into focus as her eyes adjusted to the dark. *Her* bedroom.

Cool air fluttered over her heated skin, bringing with it the sounds from the street. A car engine starting. Voices. And mirth.

She remembered not being able to fall asleep after Ben brought her home and raising the window, hoping the fresh air would do the trick. The tactic had worked, but not for long. The room was freezing.

Untangling the sheets from around her legs, she sat

up and shoved the hair out of her eyes. Now that she was awake again, she knew instinctively that sleep would again be a long time in coming.

She slid off the bed, stood up and switched on the bedside light. On bare feet, she went to the window and closed it. A paperback novel lay on her nightstand. She considered picking it up, but had tried reading before bed and couldn't concentrate. It was an old Agatha Christie novel, the various plot threads interweaving and leading to what she was sure would be a stunning climax.

She should give the book to Ben to illustrate the difference between an actual mystery and the fictional plot he'd concocted about Allison Blaine's death. All on the strength of an e-mail that libeled her father.

To think she'd actually been enjoying his company tonight. She'd have to be much more careful in the future to keep up her guard around him.

Her gaze fell on a box sitting atop the cherrywood dresser against the wall. It was filled with old photos her mother had never gotten around to putting in albums. Sierra was supposed to bring her mother the box so she could put together a collage of photos of her husband to be displayed at the festival. Sierra had been so caught up with Ben Nash that she'd left it behind on their recent visit to Mountain Village Estates.

A short time later, she was sitting at her kitchen table, a tall glass of ice water beside her as she went through the photos. Time was growing short, with the festival starting in just five days. There was no reason she couldn't do the collage herself.

The first photo she pulled out couldn't have been taken much before her father's death. It must have been summer because his skin appeared tan against the white of his lab coat, the gray hair at his temples adding a distinguished touch. Intelligence shone out of his eyes.

She traced the photo with the pads of her fingertips, blinking back the moisture in her eyes. After two years, she still missed him, still wished she would have had more time to make him proud of her.

She set the photo aside, then rummaged through the rest of the snapshots, keeping an eye out for the images that showed his philanthropic side. The minutes on the too-loud kitchen clock ticked by as she picked out photos of her father hosting a fishing tournament, handing water to competitors at a charity run and working the concession stand at a high school football game.

There were also photos of other family members, which she quickly leafed through. A flash of orange stopped her. It was the color of the cap her father wore in a photo of him standing by a golf cart. His sideburns had yet to turn gray and his face looked relatively unlined so she placed him in his forties.

She smiled, remembering the way he'd embraced the often-garish color choices seen on the golf course. Good thing he wasn't wearing his favorite pair of yellow-and-burgundy plaid pants with the orange hat.

The logo on the hat read Lakeview Pines Golf, the name of a resort in the Poconos that held a charity tournament every year in May. The photo would definitely fit in to the collage. She flipped it over to check the date, curious to see exactly how old her father had been when it was taken. The year, nineteen years in the past, made sense. The date—July sixth—did not.

A vague memory floated in her brain of the year the golf course sustained storm damage and postponed the tournament, of her parents switching their vacation plans so her father could participate.

She checked the year again. Her breath caught.

It was the same year Allison Blaine had died.

The golf course was close enough that her father would have commuted from home during the tournament. That meant her family hadn't been vacationing when Allison Blaine had gone missing and turned up dead as her mother had claimed.

And her father had been right here in Indigo Springs.

IF AT FIRST YOU don't succeed, try to get the information another way.

That had been Ben's unapologetic philosophy since he'd started his journalism career. He'd once paid a prostitute fifty bucks to tell him which cops were open to dropping a solicitation charge in exchange for sex. Another time he got a friend to offer a bribe to the head of the city planning commission on a very good hunch the official was corrupt.

He'd never before had a moment's hesitation about doing whatever it took to break a story.

So the uneasy sensation that ran through him Monday afternoon as he sat on a park bench next to Sierra's brother came as a surprise. He recognized the feeling as guilt because it was strikingly similar to what he'd experienced last night after dropping a silently fuming Sierra at her home.

Her charge that he'd had an ulterior motive in asking her out was off the mark. He couldn't deny, however, that he'd jumped at the opportunity to pump her about Quincy Coleman.

Rummaging for information so he could separate fact from fiction was what he did best. It was what he was preparing to do to her brother.

"Hope you didn't mind meeting here for lunch instead of at a restaurant." Ryan Whitmore gestured at the park that would soon be named after his father with the hand not holding his turkey club sandwich. Above where they sat on a park bench, the snowy-white blooms of a dogwood tree shaded them from the bright sun. The air smelled of freshly mowed grass and spring flowers.

"Not at all." Ben couldn't help thinking Sierra would object, not to the location, but to him meeting her brother. He guessed that Ryan hadn't shared his lunch plans with her.

"I'm cooped up all day so I like to get outside any chance I can get," Ryan added. "That river rafter I'm married to isn't the only one who appreciates the outdoors."

By the grin that spread across Ryan's face at the mention of his wife, Ben's guess was that he was a newlywed. "How long have you and Annie been married?"

"Going on three months," he said. "Our daughter's coming to live with us when school's out for the summer."

That didn't compute. "Where's your daughter now?"

"Outside of Pittsburgh with the family that adopted her." Ryan waved a hand. "It's a long story with a happy ending. Lindsey's fourteen. Old enough to decide she wanted to live with us for most of the year." He took another bite of his sandwich, then indicated the brown paper take-out bag beside Ben. "Aren't you going to eat?"

"Maybe later." He was hungrier for information than food. "Thanks, by the way, for being willing to meet."

"Why wouldn't I be?"

Ben watched two squirrels scamper across the grass and up a tree while he thought about how to answer. He went with the truth. "Your sister thinks I'm trying to tie your father to Allison Blaine's death."

Ryan's neutral expression didn't change. "Are you?"

"Somebody is. Otherwise, I wouldn't have gotten that e-mail."

Ryan chewed thoughtfully on his sandwich. Nearby a little boy of about four years old giggled wildly as a man who looked to be his father pushed his swing higher and higher.

"Have you made progress in figuring out who sent it?" Ryan asked.

"Not much," Ben said. "Any ideas?"

"The only person I know of who disliked my father is Quincy Coleman, but he seems to have had a change of heart now that Dad's gone."

"Then you know he suggested the park be re-named?"

"Not until Sierra told me this morning, I didn't. Surprised the hell out of me." He indicated a spot fifty feet away. "The signpost's going up right there, close to the sidewalk where it'll be most visible."

"Do you know why Coleman didn't get along with your father?"

"No particular reason." A bumblebee flew over to investigate what Ryan was eating. He shooed it away. "They were both prominent citizens. I think it was a case of two top dogs having problems sharing the same territory."

"Did your father have problems with anyone else?"

Ryan shook his head. "Not that I know of. He was well liked."

"Can you tell me about him? I mean, what he was really like?"

"Let's see." Ryan thought for a few moments. "He was a busy man. He was either at work or volunteering for some organization or other. The Rotary Club. The church council. The chamber of commerce. You name it, he was involved in it."

"Does that mean you and Sierra didn't see much of him?"

"I did," Ryan said. "Who do you think coached my Little League and youth basketball teams? After I got to high school, Dad never missed a game."

"How about Sierra? Was he as involved with her?"

Ryan didn't answer immediately, crumpling up the wrapper that had held his sandwich. When it was in the shape of a ball, he tossed it, sinking it into a nearby trash can on the first try. "Has Sierra told you anything about me?"

Ben could have pointed out that Ryan hadn't answered his question, but figured the other man would get around to his point eventually. He shook his head.

"We weren't close as kids. As adults, either. We barely talked until last summer when I moved back home to help her out with the practice."

"Why's that?"

"I always felt like she was competing with me. Not athletically, but in every other conceivable way. She got higher grades, went to better schools, got a more prestigious residency."

"Sounds impressive."

"Sierra is that." Unmistakable pride rang out in his voice. "She could have gotten a job anywhere she wanted. Except what she wanted was to go into practice with my father."

"Isn't that what she got?"

Ryan stared off into the distance, where the father continued to make the laughing little boy's swing arc into the air. "Yeah, but it didn't happen the way she dreamed it would. My dad was a real jerk to her when she got out of residency. He told her she wasn't ready to be a partner."

"Sounds like you don't believe that was the real reason," Ben said.

"I know it wasn't." Ryan sighed heavily. "I'm a year younger than Sierra. Dad told me he was waiting to offer the partnership to me. Except at the time I didn't want it. I had this idea about going my own way."

When Sierra had told Ben about her father, a picture had begun to take shape of a girl who adored her father. Now it crystallized into its final form, of a daughter grasping for her father's attention. "So Sierra beat you out in everything except what she most wanted."

"She got the practice," Ryan said. "We both agreed Sierra should be the one to run it after Dad died. I didn't come back on the scene until Annie and I fell back in love."

"Does Sierra know she wasn't your father's first choice?"

Ryan nodded. "She does. Hurt her bad, too. But don't get me wrong. He might not have been the best father, but he was a good man. Ask anyone."

Ben already had, although he'd been careful of how he'd extracted the information from his sources. Despite Ben's faults, he was a man of his word. He'd kept his promise to Sierra not to bring up her father's name.

There were ways around that, of course. Like any good journalist, he could guide a conversation pretty expertly.

Just this morning, a longtime Indigo Springs resident had confirmed the good things he'd been hearing about Dr. Whitmore. Teresa Bradford, a sixtyish insurance agent who had lived in Indigo Springs all her life, had brought up Dr. Whitmore because she remembered him suggesting a second collection be taken up at church to help Allison Blaine's family. She'd used the words *devoted husband, father* and *citizen* to describe him.

"I'd like to talk to Alex Rawlings." The former police chief was one of the few principle players Ben had yet to track down. "Not necessarily about your father, but about memories of the case."

"Why don't you?"

"I can't find anybody in town who knows what happened to Rawlings. The closest I came was Frank Sublinski, who remembers Rawlings retiring to Florida about fifteen years ago. He can't remember where in Florida, though."

"Fort Lauderdale," Ryan said.

"How'd you know that?"

"Alex came to my dad's funeral."

"Then you have contact information for Rawlings in Florida?" Ben asked.

"Nope," Ryan said. "But I do have an address and phone number in the Poconos. Alex moved in with a daughter who lives maybe an hour from here. I'll call you with the information when I get back to the office."

"Thanks." It didn't escape Ben's attention that one of the Whitmore siblings was much more cooperative than the other. "Out of curiosity, does Sierra know where Alex Rawlings is?"

"Oh, yeah," Ryan said and stood up. "And I don't expect her to be happy I told you."

"WHAT DID YOU SAY you did?" Sierra could barely choke out the words past the incredulity that clogged her throat.

"You heard me the first time." Ryan leaned with his back against the wall, his legs crossed at the ankles, looking fresh despite the steady stream of patients who'd kept them at work almost forty-five minutes past regular Monday office hours. "I gave Ben Nash a phone number for Alex Rawlings this afternoon."

"Why would you do that?" She'd been about to sanitize her hands from a dispenser on the wall when her brother approached. She pumped down on the device, and a too-large gob of gel squirted out.

"A better question is why wouldn't I?"

"I'll tell you why." She rubbed her hands together vigorously, using friction to dry up the gel. "Ben Nash is trying to implicate our father in that woman's death."

"So what? Nothing will come of it. Mom already told him we were on vacation when she died."

She stopped drying her hands and avoided his eyes. "He's not acting like he believes her."

There was a pregnant pause before he said, "Neither are you. What gives, Sierra?"

When had her younger brother become so perceptive? There was a time not very long ago when he hadn't known her well enough to tell what she was thinking.

"Do you remember how Dad always played in that charity golf tournament at Lakeview Pines?" she asked.

"Vaguely." He didn't have to add that their father had played in lots of charity golf tournaments. "Why?"

"One year a lightning storm took out a bunch of trees and the tournament organizers moved back the date of the tournament." She swallowed. "That was the only year we didn't go on vacation the first week in July."

"Let me guess. That was the year Allison Blaine died." At her nod, he continued in an incredulous voice, "So Mom lied."

"Of course she didn't," Sierra said quickly. "It slipped her mind. That's all. I wouldn't have remembered myself if I hadn't found an old photo of Dad with the date written on the back."

"We should tell Ben."

"No!" Sierra reached out and put a restraining hand on his arm. "We can't tell him. It'll make him even more suspicious than he already is."

"If he finds out on his own, he'll think we've got something to hide."

"Then he'd be wrong," Sierra said. "Mom made an honest mistake. Besides, Dad being in town when Allison Blaine died doesn't change anything. It still doesn't mean he knew the woman."

"Then why not tell him?"

Sierra's hand tightened on his arm. How could she make him understand? "Somebody already sent Ben an e-mail suggesting Dad was involved. We can't give him a reason to believe that's true."

"But what if Dad *was* involved?"

"What?" She stared at him openmouthed. "You know what Dad was like. How could you believe he killed somebody?"

"I don't," Ryan said quickly, "but there's obviously something suspicious about Allison Blaine's death. Maybe Dad knew what it was."

"I can't believe you're saying this! Dad's about to be honored for his charity work. He deserves better, especially from his own son."

"What about Allison Blaine's family? Don't they deserve to know what happened to her?"

"They already know. She had an accident," Sierra asserted even as a niggling doubt gnawed at her.

Would Ben Nash be going to all this trouble if it were as simple as that?

"Excuse me, but is it okay if I leave now?"

At the sound of the familiar singsong voice, they both whirled to find their receptionist standing not fifteen feet from them. How long had Missy Cromartie been there? How much had she heard?

"You don't have to ask permission to leave, Missy," Ryan said evenly.

"I know. But my car's parked out back and I didn't want to interrupt." Her face was flushed, as though from embarrassment, confirming Sierra's worst fears. She'd heard everything. "I wouldn't be here at all if I didn't need to finish up my paperwork."

"I'll walk you out," Ryan said, signaling the end of the conversation when they'd yet to settle anything.

Alone in the office, Sierra fumed silently while she wondered and worried exactly what kind of information Ben Nash would try to pull out of Alex Rawlings.

Making a snap decision, she headed in the direction her brother and Missy had just taken.

There was one sure way to find out.

ALEX RAWLINGS was a woman.

A tall woman with a sturdy build, a florid complexion, gunmetal-gray hair and a dislike for her given name of Alexandria. Ben put her age in the mid-seventies.

He'd been at her daughter's modest ranch house long enough to get settled on a back porch with a view of the wooded lawn, and he was still disappointed it hadn't occurred to him Alex was a female. It made him wonder what else about this story he wasn't seeing clearly.

"Toughest time of my life," she said in response to his question about her tenure as police chief. "People weren't as open-minded back then. Only stayed in the job a few years until I moved on."

She'd been nearly sixty by then, she explained, and ready to pack her badge away in a drawer. Yard sales had always lured her like an addict to crack so she'd jumped at the chance to help a friend peddle department store castoffs at a flea market outside of Fort Lauderdale.

"How long have you been back in Pennsylvania?" Ben asked.

"Since my heart started acting up." She sounded seriously peeved. "Doctor said if I don't take it easy, it could give out entirely. I don't believe him for a second, but Denise does."

Denise was her daughter, a younger but no less reserved version of Alex.

"Now what can I do for a hotshot like you?" Alex asked.

The screen door to the porch banged open. Ben had been half listening for it, the same way he'd been expecting the visitor who was trailing Denise. Sierra claimed she'd keep tabs on him. He was discovering she was a woman of her word.

"Sierra! What a surprise!" Ben's tone was just theatrical enough to let her know he meant the opposite.

She gave him a cool look, which matched the ice-blue color of the short-sleeved blouse she wore with a belted, matching skirt. She'd swept her long hair off her neck and secured it with a barrette. If she hadn't shown him her hot temper last night, he might buy into the frosty image she was trying to portray.

"Hey there, stranger." Alex Rawlings had a bum knee in addition to her weak heart, which had made her slow trek to the rocking chair difficult to watch. The injury didn't prevent her from standing to greet Sierra.

"Hello, Mrs. Rawlings," Sierra said.

"*Mrs. Rawlings?* Why don't you just call me *old lady.* It makes me feel just as ancient."

"Alex, then," Sierra said.

The older woman perched her hands on her hips and glowered. "Would you look at her, Denise. I haven't seen her since her father's funeral and I don't get a hug."

"You better hug her, Sierra, or you won't hear the end of it," Denise advised, a laugh in her voice.

A corner of Sierra's mouth lifted. She embraced Alex, the warmth of the act a marked difference from the frigid look she'd shot Ben when she arrived.

"That'll shut her up," Denise said. "But not for long."

"What kind of way is that for a daughter to talk to her mother?" Alex complained with a shake of her head.

"You know I love you, Mom." Denise blew her a kiss. "Why else would I be making you lemon chicken for dinner?"

Alex thrust out her lower lip unhappily. "I'd rather have lasagna with loads of cheese, but you mean well so I'll let the sassy talk slide."

Denise laughed again. "If you'll all excuse me, I need to see to dinner. You two are welcome to stay, if you like. I always make enough so we have lots of leftovers."

"Thanks," Ben said, "but I was planning to take Sierra to dinner after we're done here."

Sierra directed another glacial look his way. This one qualified as a glare. "Since when?"

He withstood the chill and winked at Denise. "As you can see, I haven't gotten around to asking her yet."

Denise cupped her hands to her mouth and spoke in a stage whisper. "If she says no, the offer of dinner stands. That way you might still find yourself sitting across the table from her."

"I think I love you," Ben told Denise.

"I'd be more fond of you, Denise, if you weren't trying to help Ben get his way," Sierra quipped.

Denise left them, her good-natured booming laugh growing softer the farther removed from them she got.

"I take it you two know each other," Alex remarked as she slowly lowered herself into her rocking chair.

"Oh, yeah." Ben remained standing, leaning against the wrought-iron porch railing. "We go way back."

"All the way back to Friday." Sierra took a seat next to Alex. "Has he told you yet why he's here?"

"We were just about to get 'round to that when you showed up." Alex gazed into the backyard, cursed, then picked up a rectangular object from beside her chair. She vigorously twirled it, emitting a racket.

He heard rustling, then caught a glimpse of the white tails of a family of deer disappearing into the woods.

"Darn deer keep eating up my flowers. I can keep

'em away with this thing when I'm out here." She held up the object in her hand, a New Year's Eve noise-maker. "But they come back when I'm asleep."

"That's because you used to buy extra apples at the orchard and leave them under the tree for the deer to eat," Denise called through the screen door.

"I thought you were making me food, girl," Alex called back. "Get cooking!"

Denise guffawed, and Ben felt himself smile. Mother and daughter had such an easy camaraderie he could see why Denise had welcomed Alex into her house. He liked to think he would have had that kind of relationship with his own mother if she'd lived. The familiar pain stabbed at him.

"Does the name Allison Blaine mean anything to you?" He was surprised his voice didn't crack when he uttered it.

"Sure does," Alex said with alacrity. "She's the tourist who fell from the overlook."

Sierra slanted him a pointed look at the police chief's wording, one of the few times she'd met his eyes since arriving.

"Mind if I ask why you remembered the incident so quickly?" Ben asked.

"In the almost two years I was police chief, only two people died. Allison Blaine and Junior Brozek, who fell off his dirt bike. Heartbreaking story, that was. Junior might have lived if he'd been wearing a helmet."

A clear-cut accident, Ben thought.

"Was there ever any thought that Allison Blaine's death wasn't an accident?" he asked.

"'Course there was," Alex answered. "Good cops don't assume anything's the way it seems. Except this was."

"How do you know?"

"We investigated. Talked to anybody who had contact with her. Found out her car had been spotted weaving near the overlook. Had her blood tested. It came back clean. Not even a drop of alcohol."

Ben wasn't surprised at the finding. He'd never known his mother to drink, not even a glass of wine at dinner. "Didn't you find it suspicious that she was up at the overlook alone when it was almost dark?"

"Not after I talked to her parents, I didn't," Alex said. "They said she liked going up there. To think, if I remember right."

It was a plausible explanation, but Ben wasn't about to swallow it whole, especially because it was possible Alex Rawlings's memory was faulty. He tried to think how to bring the conversation around to Dr. Whitmore without violating the deal he'd made with Sierra.

"Do you remember who'd been in contact with her?" he asked.

"It was a long time ago." Alex scratched her gray head and squinted in thought. "Her parents, naturally. And those people who used to own Jimmy's Diner. Elderly couple. They sold the place a couple years after I left town."

She was talking about Gladys and Andy Stack, both of whom had passed away years ago. They'd been close friends of Ben's maternal grandparents, who'd moved to Indigo Springs in part to help out at the restaurant.

"I met her once, too," Alex announced.

Ben straightened from the railing, his news sense on alert.

"It was at the restaurant. She had a couple of kids with her. I only remember the littlest because he was a hellion. She was chasing him all over the place. Made me tired watching her."

Connor Nash, Ben's youngest brother, had been four at the time. He'd gone on to become one of the speediest high school running backs in the Philadelphia area, playing with a reckless style that made him hard to tackle.

"Did my father know her?" Sierra asked the question in a firm, steady voice.

"Not that I remember," Alex said.

To Sierra's credit, she didn't give Ben another knowing look.

"Wouldn't have been any reason for them to cross paths unless she got sick when she was in town," Alex added.

"She didn't," Sierra said. "We already checked Dad's records."

"That's right. You and your brother took over his practice, didn't you?" Alex's expression grew wistful. "Shame he's gone. He was a fine doctor, but even a finer man. Did you know he was the reason I was police chief at all?"

"What do you mean?" Sierra asked.

"Like I was telling Ben here before you showed up, people weren't real accepting of a female police chief twenty years ago. When word got out I was up for the job, some of the town bigwigs tried to stop it. Probably would have if Dr. Whitmore hadn't stood up for me."

"I didn't know that," Sierra said quietly.

"Dr. Whitmore didn't go around singing his own praises," Alex said. "That's one of the reasons I loved that man."

"Thank you for telling me, Alex," Sierra said softly.

Ben bit back the question that sprang to mind, knowing it would incense Sierra and probably insult Alex.

He couldn't help hearing it shouted in his brain, though.

If Alex felt that way about Dr. Whitmore, how likely was she to suspect him of any wrongdoing?

CHAPTER SEVEN

LATER THAT NIGHT Sierra felt herself tottering and hooked the heel of her shoe on the bottom of her bar stool to steady herself.

"The people in here falling out of their chairs usually have more than one drink." Chuck Dudza, the sixtyish owner of the Blue Haven Pub, paused in the act of wiping down the bar. He nodded to the glass of mineral water she was nursing. "And they're always drinking something stronger than that."

She squirmed on the stool while she breathed in air that smelled of beer and peanuts. The darn thing really should have a back rest. "I didn't think it was that noticeable."

"What? That you're uncomfortable being in here all by your lonesome? Yeah, it is." He resumed his vigorous wiping while her gaze swept the bar, checking to see who else had noticed her uneasiness. Ben Nash, sitting at a table with the father and son who ran Pollock Construction, raised his glass to her. She quickly looked away.

"What brings you here tonight anyway, Doc?" Chuck asked. "I've only seen you in here before with that pharmacist."

So Chuck hadn't been in the bar Friday night when

she'd sauntered in with her tight clothes and high heels and would have made a fool of herself if Ben hadn't been so sweet.

She shoved the favorable thought of Ben from her mind, aware it was the second time her subconscious tried to give the infernal man points for being a decent human being. The verdict on that was still out.

"I need to talk to Jill about the festival." It wasn't the primary reason for her visit, but neither was it a lie. She and Jill were collaborating on the volunteer schedule. "Is she working tonight?"

"She's on break." Chuck glanced up at the red numbers on the neon clock above the rows of hanging glasses. "She should have been back fifteen minutes ago. That's unlike her."

Three young men who looked like they'd spent the day in the sun, probably hiking or rafting, approached the bar from one side. A couple closed in from the other direction.

"I'd check on her if I wasn't the only one tending bar," Chuck said.

"I'll do it," Sierra offered. It beat watching Ben Nash chat up Nick and Johnny Pollock. "Any idea where I should look?"

"Maybe at the park," Chuck said. "She likes to go there when the weather's good. You can take the exit by the restrooms. It's shorter."

Being careful not to lose her balance, Sierra got down from the tall stool. Ben was listening to something Nick Pollock said, nodding intently, his attention focused on the older man.

Was it possible Nick Pollock would remember her father had not been at the Jersey shore when Allison Blaine died?

He was about the age her father would have been had he lived. Yet Sierra had no idea if he'd known her father well enough to remember a detail like that.

Temporarily putting the problem out of her mind, she went in search of Jill, taking the path Chuck indicated.

The bar was only about a third full, but that was more of a crowd than Sierra had expected for a Monday night. The clientele seemed to be made up mostly of tourists. One of them, a woman in her early twenties wearing a very short, tight dress, pressed some buttons on the jukebox. Beyoncé started to sing and the woman lifted her arms overhead and gyrated suggestively to the music.

Every man in the bar would probably risk whiplash to ogle her. Sierra looked around to test her theory. Ben Nash wasn't watching the woman. His eyes were on her.

Trying not to show that his gaze disconcerted her, she kept her chin high and walked deliberately toward the abbreviated hallway. When an interior wall was between her and Ben Nash's sight line, she felt her shoulders sag. She hurried the rest of the way to the exit, then let herself out through the alleyway. A short walk later and she was in the park.

At first she thought she was alone, but then she spied a lone figure sitting on the edge of the amphitheater stage. Her head was bowed, her dark hair forming a curtain over her face. It was Jill.

Fallen leaves and small twigs crunched underneath Sierra's feet, but Jill didn't seem to hear her approach.

"Jill?" Sierra ventured.

The other woman's head jerked up. Her face was almost entirely in darkness, but Sierra picked up on the bleakness of her expression. In a flash, the desolation was gone.

"Hey there, Sierra. What are you doing out here?" Jill greeted her like an old friend, even though they'd never exchanged more than a few words at a time. "Oh, wait a minute. I forgot to send you an e-mail with the names of the festival volunteers so you could do the schedule."

"You can send me the e-mail tomorrow," Sierra said. "That'll be plenty of time."

"Better yet, I'll do the schedule. It's the least I can do after messing up." Jill cocked her head, as though a thought had just occurred to her. "How did you know to look for me in the park?"

"Chuck suggested it when I offered to check on you," she said. "Your break ended fifteen minutes ago."

"Oh, my goodness. Is it really that late? The time really got away from me." Jill lengthened her vowels, the drawl in her voice marking her as a Southerner.

There was something else in her voice, too. A thickness that wasn't normally present. Sierra looked closer and thought she saw traces of tears on Jill's face.

It's none of your business, a familiar voice inside her head advised. *You have enough problems of your own without getting involved in someone else's.*

"It sure was good of you to hunt me down." The

trembling at the corners of Jill's mouth dimmed her smile. "I need to be getting back or Chuck'll think I died."

"Do you want to talk about what's bothering you first?" Sierra asked gently.

Jill blinked a few times. "What makes you think something's bothering me?"

Sierra glanced down at her blue outfit, which was such a light shade it would easily soil, and shrugged. That was what dry cleaners were for. She climbed the few short steps to the amphitheater stage and lowered herself next to Jill. "You don't strike me as a woman who sits alone in the dark."

Jill's entire body seemed to sag. "I yelled at my brother."

"Is that all?" Sierra asked. "I've yelled at my brother lots of times. Why, I let Ryan have it just this afternoon."

Jill shook her head. "You don't understand. Your brother's about your age. Mine's only ten. He lives with me."

Sierra wondered why the boy resided with Jill, but asking her to explain would be getting off a topic the other woman obviously needed to discuss. "What did he do?"

"He was playing with his remote control car in front of the house." She took a deep breath. The smell of damp grass was in the air. "It got stuck on a curb and he ran across the street, directly in front of a truck. When those brakes squealed, I must've lost a year of my life."

"Sounds like your brother had a talking-to coming." Sierra didn't have to be an expert on raising children to realize how important it was to stress safety.

"Except I went way beyond a talking-to." Jill looked miserable. "My brother's been through a rough time. I know he's not the kind of kid you should yell at and I still lost my temper."

Again, Sierra suppressed her curiosity about her friend's young brother and focused on how to help her. "So you're usually perfect?"

Jill emitted a surprised sound. "Of course not. I mess up all the time."

"Me, too." Sierra thought about her propensity to let down her guard around Ben Nash when she knew his main reason for being around her was to extract information. "This is just a guess, but I bet you've never yelled at your brother before."

"Not that I can remember," Jill said.

"Then apologize," Sierra advised.

"I already did, and he's still not talking to me."

"Did you tell him how scared you were when you thought that truck might hit him?" Sierra asked.

Jill didn't respond for a moment. "Not in so many words."

"Then do." Sierra took Jill's hand and squeezed it. "I think you'll find people can forgive a great many things when they're done in the name of love."

WELL, THAT WAS ANOTHER dead end in a town that was full of them.

Ben had arranged to meet Nick Pollock over dinner

at the pub, having heard from a number of town residents he'd been actively involved in the community for thirty years.

Nick's son Johnny had joined them. Although the younger Pollock was a child at the time of his mother's death, Ben had viewed the meeting as doubling the odds of discovering new information.

The odds hadn't played out.

He picked up the bill on the table. He'd told his dinner companions the newspaper would reimburse him for his cost. In truth he had no intention of turning in an expense report, not when the story was personal and his boss wanted him to drop it.

"If you haven't found anything by now, there's nothing to find," Joe Geraldi had said earlier that afternoon when he'd called to check on Ben's progress. "I need you back here working on that group home story."

Ben had bought himself more time by saying he had a few more people to talk to. He'd paid Quincy Coleman a visit, confirming what Sierra and Ryan had already told him. Then he'd set out to ferret out what the Pollocks knew, which was a big fat nothing.

He started to sign his name on the credit card slip when the day and the month on the filmy white paper registered. It wasn't today's date that was significant, but tomorrow's.

On a subliminal level, he must have known the date was approaching. Along with his lack of progress on the story that meant so much to him, it explained why he'd grown more melancholy as the night wore on.

He tapped his fingers on the tabletop, trying to figure out why his usual methods weren't working.

He couldn't accept it was because there was nothing to discover. There had to be a reason "mountain-dweller" had sent the e-mail, an explanation for why his gut had always rejected the tale of how his mother died.

Feeling a headache coming on, he rubbed the bridge of his nose. For one of the first times in his career, he wasn't sure what his next step should be.

Some reporter he was. He'd even lost track of Sierra.

One minute she'd been trying not to counterbalance on that bar stool, and the next she was disappearing down the hall that led to the restrooms.

When the minutes lengthened without her returning, it finally dawned on him there must be a rear exit. So tonight of all nights, he didn't even have Sierra as a distraction.

And then Sierra emerged from the hall with the curly-haired bartender. Jill, he believed her name was.

Their heads were close together, their bodies angled toward each other as though deep in conversation. Just shy of the bar, Jill gave Sierra a warm hug before getting back to work.

Odd. He hadn't realized the two women were friends.

He was at Sierra's side before she could reclaim the stool from where she'd been watching him earlier in the evening. "You're not real good at keeping tabs on me."

She tossed her brown hair, which was now hanging

long and loose the way he liked it. She perched her hands on her hips before saying airily, "Is that so?"

Incredibly, he felt a smile coming on. "It is so. I could have left the bar and you wouldn't know where I went."

"You didn't leave," she pointed out.

"Ah, but you would be in a far better keeping-tabs position if you'd accepted my dinner invitation. Then you'd know everything the Pollocks told me."

Her gaze narrowed. "What did they tell you?"

Nick Pollock had informed him Dr. Whitmore had been integral in lobbying the city to erect a guard rail at the site where Ben's mother died. Pollock then proceeded to call Dr. Whitmore a good man, adding his voice to the multitudes.

"Nothing of note," Ben said.

"Good. Then maybe you'll give it a rest."

Not likely.

"I am kind of tired," he said, deliberately misunderstanding. He yawned for effect. "I'm calling it a night. Want to keep tabs on me when I walk to the hotel?"

She hesitated, and he felt a no coming his way.

"You never know who I might run into or what they might tell me," he added.

Her mouth twisted and he could almost see her mind working. "In that case," she said haughtily, "I accept."

He ended up walking her home, insisting upon it even though she assured him the downtown area was safe after dark. Late on a Monday night, activity was nearly nonexistent except for the occasional car and the call of a distant night bird. The tourists who visited

Indigo Springs tended to be the early-to-bed, early-to-rise types.

"You know what I don't get," she said when they'd almost reached her doorstep. "I don't get why the story's so important to you."

"Every story's important to me," he said without inflection.

She nodded, accepting his lame explanation. She came to a stop in front of her door, in much the same way as she had that first night they'd met.

That night, he'd been reasonably confident she'd let him kiss her. He had no cause for optimism tonight.

"What?" Her back was to the streetlight, her face partially in shadows. He knew her expressions well enough by now he could tell her nose was wrinkled and her lips thinned. "You're not going to try to get me to invite you in?"

"Not tonight," he said.

"Is something wrong?" She sounded less suspicious, almost...concerned. "You don't seem yourself tonight."

He shrugged, surprised she'd picked up on his mood when he was trying so hard to conceal it. He tried to throw her off track. "You don't know me well enough to say that."

"Maybe not, but I can tell something's bothering you." She chewed on her lower lip. "Look. I know I've been giving you a hard time, but you helped me out when I was in a jam, and, well, I can be a good listener."

Since he'd signed the credit-card slip, it had felt as though the weight of tomorrow's date was pressing on his shoulders. He had a crazy premonition the burden wouldn't be as hard to bear if he shared it.

"I realized earlier this evening that Wednesday is my mother's birthday." He seldom spoke about his mother because it was just so damn hard to talk about her without his voice breaking. He struggled for control. "It brought home how miserably I was letting her down."

She tilted her head quizzically, her expression softening. "If you forgot to get her a present, there's still time to send flowers."

He took a deep breath and released it before speaking. "My mother died when I was twelve years old."

"She did?" Surprise made her voice sound higher than normal. "I had the impression she and your father were divorced."

"That's what I wanted you to believe."

"Why?"

"A little while ago you asked why the story was so important to me." He wet his suddenly dry lips, unable to come up with a reason to continue to keep his secret. "It's important because Allison Blaine was my mother."

He waited for her to chastise him for keeping that pertinent piece of information to himself. The silence between them stretched, the hoot of what sounded like an owl filling it.

She was holding her key ring in her right hand, having fished it out of her purse as they walked through the downtown. Wordlessly, she inserted one of the keys into the lock and opened the door.

Just when he thought she'd disappear inside without saying anything, she turned and held the door open wide.

"Why don't you come in?"

SIERRA WALKED SLOWLY into her living room, careful not to spill either of the mugs of decaf she balanced in her hands. She suspected Ben didn't want the coffee any more than she did, but offering him a beverage had given her a chance to collect her thoughts.

She didn't know why she hadn't guessed Allison Blaine was Ben's mother, especially because that simple fact explained so much.

"Here you go." She delivered the coffee to where he sat in one of the room's two large swivel chairs. Their fingers brushed, and she resisted the impulse to wrap her hand around his and hang on.

"Thanks." He watched her sit on the matching love seat, then swept a hand to indicate the small room where she spent most of her time. "I like your style."

The swivel chairs flanked the love seat. She'd chosen a burnt-orange fabric to pick up the warmth of the wood floor. She'd piled multicolored pillows on the furniture and added modern glass end tables and funky lamps with zigzag bases. The walls were painted a pale ginger, and pleated shades topped with tricolor valances covered the windows. A plasma screen television was mounted over the fireplace.

"I guess both of us are full of surprises," she said.

"I didn't say I was surprised." Although it didn't take much movement for his chair to swivel, it remained perfectly still. "The room suits you."

She doubted anyone else in her acquaintance would say that. Now wasn't the time to talk about her taste in decorating, though.

"Then you're the surprising one," she said. "Why do you have a different last name than your mother?"

"Blaine was her maiden name. She kept it when she married my father."

Sierra thought that was odd, considering the times, but there were other issues to explore more important than whether his mother was an early feminist. "Why didn't you say something before now about Allison Blaine being your mother?"

He leaned his head back against the pillows and looked at a point on the ceiling instead of at her. "It's hard to explain. I guess I thought I could keep my emotions out of it if I treated it like any other story."

"Except that's not working out," she said softly.

"Not by a long shot," he acknowledged, then grew silent.

She'd never been one to pry in another person's affairs, but something he'd told her made her go against her long-held practice.

"That one time you visited Indigo Springs," she asked quietly, "was it when your mother died?"

"Yeah," he said after a moment. "She brought me and my two younger brothers to visit our grandparents. Her parents."

She felt his pain as acutely as if it were her own. "That must have been a terrible time for all of you."

"I'm quite a bit older than my brothers. They didn't really understand what was happening."

"How about you?"

"I was plenty old enough to know she was never coming back." He paused. "After all these years, I still miss her."

"What was she like?"

"She was a mom. Sweet. Quiet. Always there when you needed her even though she had to work hard to make ends meet."

Again he lapsed into silence. Again she felt he might stop talking if she didn't keep asking questions. "What did she do for a living?"

"She worked at the day care where she sent my brothers. When my father was home, which wasn't often because he was a truck driver, she'd work a second job at night. She was on a cleaning crew, I'm pretty sure at an office building."

He reached into his wallet and pulled out a photo worn around the edges. It depicted a young boy she instantly recognized as Ben smiling directly into the camera. A pretty, dark-haired woman with large, dark eyes rested her chin on top of his head, her arms encircling him. An enormous gray creature was in the background.

"Is that a hippopotamus?"

A corner of his mouth quirked. "For some reason, I was crazy about them. On my tenth birthday, she took half a day off work and picked me up after school. She didn't tell me where we were going until we got to the Pittsburgh zoo."

"She looks so young," Sierra said.

"She was only thirty when she died. A little younger

than I am now. She was seventeen when she married my dad," he said. "I didn't find out until after she died they got married because she was pregnant."

"That must have been tough." Sierra had seen the complications of teenage pregnancy firsthand last summer when her niece—the daughter Ryan and Annie had given up for adoption when they were in their teens—had shown up unannounced in Indigo Springs. "Did your mother finish high school?"

"No," Ben said. "That's something else I found out after she was gone. It explained why she took the types of jobs she did, although at the time I didn't realize how tough it must have been for her. She never complained."

"She sounds wonderful." Sierra handed the photo back to him. "I'm glad you and your brothers have such warm memories of her."

"I'm afraid my brothers don't remember her very well," he said. "Like I told you before, my dad got re-married before I went off to college. My brothers call our stepmother Mom." He paused long enough for her to suspect he'd clammed up for good this time, but then he said in an even softer voice, "It's almost like they've forgotten her."

She remembered him saying he had stayed in Pittsburgh year-round while he attended college. None of the newspapers at which he'd mentioned working were near Philadelphia, where his father and stepmother lived.

"Do you see your family much?" she asked.

"On the occasional holiday if I'm not working," he said. "Jerry and Connor—those are my brothers—

settled in the Philadelphia area. They're both married with kids."

A picture crystallized of a man determinedly keeping himself apart from family. She could hear distance in his voice when he talked about them.

"Maybe your brothers didn't forget your mother," she said gently. "Maybe they're just getting on with their lives. Maybe that's what you should do, too."

He blew out a heavy breath through a narrow space between his lips. "That's what my boss suggested, too."

Sierra wasn't consciously aware of scooting forward and reaching out to him until her hand rested on his knee. He covered her hand with his, sending warmth shooting through her. Then he turned it over so their palms were touching and interlaced their fingers.

Their eyes met. Her animosity disappeared as though it had never been. She would swear their connection went a level deeper than the physical.

"I should be going." He didn't make any move to get up. The lines around his eyes looked more pronounced than usual. She put the cause at fatigue, disappointment or possibly a combination of the two. She imagined him returning to his lonely room at the Indigo Inn, where he'd lie awake thinking about how his mother's birthday was getting inexorably closer.

Without letting go of him, she got up from the love seat and tugged on his hand until he was standing, too.

"I'd like it better if you stayed," she whispered.

Mere days ago when she'd first gotten the idea to proposition him, her hands had shaken so much she'd had trouble getting dressed. Tonight the hand that he still held was as steady as her voice.

His forehead wrinkled as he regarded her. "Are you sure?"

"Very sure."

He still didn't look convinced. She anchored the hand not holding his on his shoulder and moved closer to him, until their upper bodies touched.

She heard his sharp intake of breath just before she raised her lips and kissed him. He barely moved, allowing her lips to play with his as she experimented with soft, feathery kisses.

She couldn't remember ever seizing the initiative in a sexual situation, not even as a teenager. In her years with Chad, he'd always taken the lead.

Ben's hand tightened around hers. She moved closer to him and felt the evidence of his arousal. A thrill ran through her that she'd done that to him with the slightest of kisses.

She moved her hand from his shoulder to his nape, holding his head in place. Her heartbeat quickened, then she very deliberately parted his lips with her tongue.

She delved inside, enjoying the nubby texture of his tongue and the heat that seemed to start at her mouth and spread. He tasted both like the beer he'd drunk at the Blue Haven, and like himself. Clean and warm and masculine, the way he smelled.

Her tongue mated with his, kissing him deeply as an urgency built inside her. Their elbows were bent, their hands still linked and pressed between their bodies, against their hearts.

She angled her mouth to kiss him even more deeply, reveling in the feel of his slightly scratchy beard against her skin. She couldn't seem to get close enough to him. She ran her free hand down the length of his back, pressing her body closer to his erection. He willingly participated, seemingly content to let her move at her own pace.

The tension built inside her, begging for release. She pulled her mouth from his, finding the act as difficult as if she were a starving bear lapping at honey. She felt dazed when she looked at him—and amazed she could feel this way from mere kisses.

She stepped back from him, finding it convenient that she was still holding his hand. She nodded up the stairs. "My bedroom's that way."

Her voice sounded sultry and smoky and unfamiliar. At the same time she felt as though a part of her had been buried below the surface, waiting for a chance to emerge.

She was conscious of every sensation as she led him to her bedroom. The tap of their heels on the hardwood floor. The quick beat of her heart. The breaths that were coming too fast.

Mostly she was aware of what would happen next. The knowledge reached every pore of her body, as though her veins were filled with anticipation instead of blood.

Her bedroom was her favorite room in the house. She'd indulged her every whim in decorating it, favoring a white lacy theme for the bedspread and curtains.

She switched on the light, the glow highlighting

how aggressively masculine he looked in the feminine space.

He looked just right.

She let go of his hand, gave him a gentle push so he sat on the bed and then did something she'd never done in front of another person.

She stripped.

His eyes, hot and intense, didn't leave her as she slowly unbuttoned her blouse. Her heart hammered, her fingers shook and her hand stilled before she could finish. She moistened her suddenly desert-dry lips, wondering why she thought she could go through with this.

Then his eyes met hers, and he nodded. The movement was almost imperceptible, but it was enough.

She finished unbuttoning her blouse and shrugged out of it, letting it drop to the floor. Her hands were more sure now, her breathing a little more even. She unzipped her skirt and shimmied it down her hips until she wore only a push-up bra and lacy, barely there panties.

His eyes were no less intense but there was a lift to the corners of his mouth.

"Hot damn," he said.

It was the most amazing thing, really. Standing in front of him in only her high heels and underwear, she should have felt like she was reenacting a scene in a bad movie.

Instead she felt…happy. Really, really turned on. And unable to move.

"I think I just lost my nerve," she said.

He rose from the bed and pulled his shirt over his

head. His chest was sculpted with lean muscle and the perfect amount of hair.

He walked toward her with an easy, sexy grace. His hands felt big and warm on her bare skin, his lips soft and thrilling where they grazed her cheek.

"You did great," he said, moving his mouth so it hovered above hers. "I can take it from here."

She raised her lips and let him.

CHAPTER EIGHT

A FAMILIAR TUNE slowly invaded Ben's consciousness, pulling him out of sleep as the previous night came back to him.

Sierra standing in front of him, wearing the lacy bra and panties that would have made her look like a pin-up model if she hadn't been gazing at him so shyly.

Advancing until he could touch her, unhooking her bra, slipping off her panties, running his hands over her warm, sleek skin, taking her back to bed and making love to her.

A delicious languor filled him. His eyes still closed, he turned and reached for her. All he encountered were cool sheets and empty space.

He cracked open his eyelids to confirm what he already knew. He was alone. Except that wasn't quite accurate.

The tune was still playing. It dawned on him it was coming from the television in Sierra's living area. Now that he was fully awake, he easily identified it as the theme from *SportsCenter.*

Scratching his head, he sat up and swung his legs off the bed. He pulled on his jeans and one of the beaters he typically wore under his shirts, then walked soundlessly into the main part of the town house on bare feet.

Sierra sat on one of her funky swivel chairs with her legs tucked under her, fully dressed in navy slacks and a short-sleeved, lightweight pink sweater. Her hair was damp, supposedly from the shower she'd already taken. She cradled a coffee cup in both hands, her attention riveted on the TV screen. Alex Rodriguez, the third baseman for the Yankees, dove for a ground ball, then fired from his knees, throwing the runner out at first.

"Good play," Ben said.

Sierra's body jerked, the coffee sloshing in her cup. She swiveled her chair to regard him. "I didn't hear you come into the room." She grimaced, one of her hands covering her mouth. "Oh, no. The volume's on too loud, isn't it? Did it wake you?"

"Hey, the only thing better than waking up to *SportsCenter* would be waking up to *SportsCenter* with you in bed beside me."

The natural glow of her skin immediately tinged with pink. He smiled, amazed and charmed that words could make a woman who'd done a striptease blush.

"I think you better give me that coffee cup." He moved toward her, extending a hand.

"Why?" she asked, even as she obliged.

He set the coffee cup down, bent, anchored his hands about two feet apart on the back of the chair and kissed her.

He felt her intake of breath when their mouths met. She tasted like the coffee she'd just drunk, but sweet instead of bitter. He gently drew her bottom lip into his mouth, the way he'd discovered she liked.

He lifted a hand to stroke her face. Without both of his hands steadying it, the chair spun halfway around. Her mouth twisted away from his. She craned her head, her shocked eyes meeting his before she let loose with a full-bodied laugh that started in her diaphragm and expanded outward.

"You think that's funny, do you?" he asked.

She nodded, her eyes crinkling at the corners. "I've heard about kisses that make your head spin," she said through her laughter, "but this is the first time I've experienced it."

He laughed with her, shocked that he could easily identify the emotion running through him. It was happiness. Instant remorse coursed through him that he could feel happy the day before his mother's birthday in the town where she'd died.

"There's room enough for two," Sierra said, moving over in the now-stable chair and patting the space beside her.

He took her invitation, carefully lowering himself to join her. Still, the chair spun round. She laughed again. Just like that, his sorrow disappeared.

"If Rafael Nadal didn't already deserve the title," she said, naming a top tennis player who was known for the heavy topspin he put on the ball, "I'd call you the spin master."

"A sports analogy from the woman watching the best show on television," he said. "Nice. I'm starting to like you more and more."

She smiled at him, running a hand over the stubble on his lower face. "Clear something up for me. How can it look like you always need a shave yet you don't develop a beard?"

"I use an electric razor," he said, "but I don't bother putting on shaving cream or even wetting my skin."

"Because you like the no-shave look?"

"Because I'm too lazy to bother," he said, grinning. "I'm not a morning person."

"Me, neither. I use *SportsCenter* to help me wake up." She smelled of coffee, toothpaste, shampoo and her scented moisturizer, diverse scents that somehow worked together. "I can't start the day without the West Coast scores."

"So you're a baseball fan?"

She snuggled against him. "I'm a pro sports fan. Baseball, basketball, football, soccer, ice hockey. You're lucky to live in a city with good pro sports teams."

"Don't I know it," he said. "Tickets are tough to get for the Steelers and Penguins, but I have a friend who works for a ticket broker. He can get me deals on concerts, too."

"I love going to concerts," she said. "And plays. Oh. And the symphony and the opera."

"Ah-ha," he said. "A big-city girl at heart. So what are you doing in Indigo Springs?"

They were sitting so close he felt her body jerk in surprise. "This is where I live. This is home."

"It doesn't seem like a good fit for you," he said.

"It's home," she repeated stubbornly.

"Any time you're in Pittsburgh," he said, "I'll take you wherever you want to go."

"C'mon, Ben." She cut her eyes at him. "We both know I'm not coming to visit you."

He felt himself frown. "How do we both know that?"

"The same way we both know this isn't real."

He ran his hand up and down her arm, enjoying the way she sighed in pleasure. "You feel real."

"Okay, *real* wasn't the right word. I should have said *temporary*." She emphasized the last word in the sentence. "We both know this is temporary."

His impulse was to argue with her, but that was ridiculous. Of course their relationship, however satisfying, wouldn't last. He'd eventually return to Pittsburgh, and she'd stay in Indigo Springs, probably for the rest of her life.

But he was here now—and so was she.

No matter how much pressure his boss applied, he wasn't going anywhere until he found out who sent that e-mail. To that end, he could spend the day recanvassing ground he'd already covered, looking for something he might have missed.

Or he could put the story on hold and indulge himself—with Sierra.

"What do you say we make the most of the time we do have?" he asked. "How about you taking the day off?"

"I couldn't do that!" She sounded like he'd suggested she hack off her arm.

"Why not? When's the last time you called in?"

Her hesitation told him it had been a very long time. "That's not the point," she said. "I couldn't put Ryan in that spot. There's way too much work for one person."

He withdrew his arm from around her and managed to get his cell phone out of his jeans pocket. "We'll see about that."

He pressed some keys, navigating to the phone number he wanted, glad he'd asked for it.

"What are you doing?" she asked.

He held up a finger while the phone was answered on the other end. "Ryan? Ben Nash here. Would it be okay if Sierra took the day off?"

Her eyes formed the shape of the baseball that was currently being hit out of the park on *SportsCenter.* She grabbed for the phone, but he angled his body, easily keeping it away from her while he listened to Ryan's response.

"You can? Great. Thanks, man." He hung up, taking advantage of her temporary muteness to explain, "He said he'll call the nurse practitioner who works with you. She told him just yesterday she wanted to pick up some more hours."

"But…but…" she sputtered. "What must he think?"

"He probably thinks it's about time his sister had some fun." He continued before she could protest further. "I've got to shower and get a change of clothes at the hotel, but after that I'm all yours. So what do you want to do? Whitewater rafting? Mountain biking?"

Her mouth opened and closed, as though she wasn't sure whether to keep protesting. "I like to watch sports, but I'm not very athletic," she finally said. "I try to keep in shape, but outdoor sports aren't my thing."

He noticed the exercise bike in the corner of the room, the Wii Fit beside her television.

"Then how about a hike?" he asked. "You can handle that much outdoors, can't you?"

"Of course I can," she said. "I'm just not real sure I can handle you."

"Oh, but you can," he said in a suggestive voice. "Now that you don't have to go to work, I'll let you handle me before we go on that hike."

She rolled her eyes. "That's a really lame line."

"I know," he said. "But did it work?"

The corners of her mouth twitched, betraying the smile she was fighting.

"All I ask is that you be gentle with me," he said.

Her smile broke free. Since they were already touching from shoulder to thigh, it didn't take much maneuvering before they were in each other's arms, with the passion of their kisses accelerating with dizzying speed.

Ben couldn't say for certain who made the first move. If pressed, he'd say they both had.

"YOU DID NOT!" Sierra laughed up at Ben, her eyes sparkling. The Tuesday afternoon sun bathed the downtown of Indigo Springs in light, bringing out the healthy glow of her skin.

"Sure did," Ben said. "I told the managing editor I wouldn't take the job at the *Tribune* without a guarantee I could veto assignments."

"But you just said it was your dream job to be an investigative reporter."

"It is. That's why I made sure I wouldn't find myself covering the school board or writing obits."

"Why would you take a chance like that when newspapers all over the country are struggling? What if he'd said no?"

"He didn't."

Sierra's ponytail swung when she shook her head. She was dressed more informally than he'd ever seen her, in khaki shorts, a Massachusetts General Hospital T-shirt and tennis shoes. "I couldn't gamble like that."

He cupped his hand under her elbow. "Maybe you should."

"Maybe I am." Her eyes danced. "I'm with you, aren't I?"

He could have pointed out she was hardly taking a risk, considering the fleeting nature of their relationship, but didn't want to think about that. Not today when he had her to himself.

They were on their way to the printer to pick up updated fliers. After their hike Sierra had gotten a call from Quincy Coleman explaining the originals had the festival ending on Monday instead of Sunday. Coleman had heard she wasn't at work and asked if she could pick up the new flyers and distribute them. Ben had readily offered to help.

"The printer's name is Mr. Porter," Sierra told him as they approached the shop. "Don't let him fool you. He seems like a crusty old man, but underneath he's a sweetheart."

Ben held the door open for her, then stepped inside a small shop dominated by copy machines and shelves filled with packages of paper. The smell of ink assaulted him. Behind a long, narrow counter at the back of the shop was a man on the far end of seventy. He was stoop-shouldered with wisps of white hair barely covering his scalp.

"About time somebody got here. Those flyers have been ready since this morning," the man bit out. Mr. Porter, Ben presumed. "Who's that with you, Sierra?"

"This is Ben Nash." Sierra walked with Ben toward the counter. Up close, the man seemed smaller but no less animated. "Ben, this is Mr. Porter. He's been running Porter's Printing since I was a girl."

"I only regret I waited until my fifties to do it," he said as he pumped Ben's hand. "I bought this place eighteen years ago after I quit the most god-awful, boring job known to man."

"Accountant?" Ben guessed, picking a math-intensive profession. He had little affinity for the subject.

"What kind of damn fool guess is that?" Mr. Porter scoffed, shaking his head. "A bank teller. I was never more glad to get away from a place. And then there's Quincy Coleman, to this day telling me I should have stayed on longer, that old fool."

Ben chuckled. "Looks like you've made a good business for yourself."

"Used to be a *great* business before newspapers started losing circulation. My printing press hardly gets a workout." He inclined his head toward Ben. "You must know all about that, being in the business yourself."

"How do you know I work for a newspaper?" Ben asked.

"Not much gets by me," he said. "I heard you're working on a story about Allison."

Ben's heart stuttered at Mr. Porter's use of his mother's first name. "Did you know her?" he asked, his voice sharper than he'd intended.

"Not enough to be of any help to you, I'm afraid," Mr. Porter said.

Ben struggled to keep from demanding Mr. Porter immediately tell him everything he knew. "I'd like to hear whatever you do remember about her."

The old man stared at Ben through eyes narrowed behind his glasses. It seemed a long time before he said, "You're her son, aren't you?"

Ben cocked his head curiously. "How did you know that?"

"Why else would you be so interested in something that happened twenty years ago?" he asked. "Besides, the apple doesn't fall far from the tree."

Before his mother's death, strangers had commented on their resemblance. Even afterward, family members and friends mentioned it. Nobody had noted the likeness in a very long time. "You must have known her fairly well if you remember what she looked like."

"I remember because she was a beautiful woman. And because of those posters of her," he said. "I only met her the one time."

Once could be enough to get Ben's investigation on track. "When was that?"

"When she came into the bank," he said. "Broke up

the boredom, I'll tell you that much. She asked about opening an account."

"For my grandparents?" At the printer's blank look, Ben clarified, "Leonard and Barbara Blaine. They were her parents."

"I know who they were," Mr. Porter said. "They used to come into the bank themselves. They didn't need their daughter opening an account for them."

"You just said that was the reason she was in the bank," Ben said.

"Pay attention, son. I said she asked about opening an account. For herself. 'Cept she didn't. Something to do with not having the minimum balance to avoid fees."

It made sense that his mother couldn't come up with the minimum balance. It didn't compute that she'd need a local bank account—unless she planned to leave his father and relocate to Indigo Springs. Except that didn't add up, either. He didn't recall his parents ever sharing an angry word and specifically remembered his mother telling him they were visiting.

"Are you sure?" Ben asked.

"As sure as I can be about anything after twenty years," Mr. Porter said. "She went missing the very next day. A shame, it was. I always felt bad I didn't help in the search."

"Why didn't you?"

"I was golfing. Before I hurt my back, I was always playing in some tournament or another," he said. "I spent too much time on the nineteenth hole. By the time I got home, the search had been called off on account of darkness. Frank Sublinski found her body the next day."

Mr. Porter kept talking, telling Ben how sorry he was that his mother had died the way she did, mouthing platitudes about what a nice woman she'd been.

Ben accepted the comments in silence, acknowledging them with a slow nod that felt weighed down by sadness.

"You about ready for those fliers, Sierra?" Mr. Porter asked.

The printer's use of Sierra's name snapped Ben back to the present. He'd been so engrossed in finding out what Mr. Porter knew he'd nearly forgotten Sierra was standing next to him.

"I'm ready," Sierra said.

Ben touched her lightly on the back while the printer got the stack of fliers together. She met his gaze briefly, all of the earlier levity in her eyes gone. That was unsurprising considering she knew tomorrow was his mother's birthday.

It all cycled back to his mother.

His chance conversation with Mr. Porter gave him another avenue to explore. Ben could get back in touch with Quincy Coleman, the retired president of the local bank, to see if he remembered Ben's mother stopping by. He could also visit the library again and possibly jog someone's memory about who'd been using the computers when mountaindweller sent the e-mail.

For now, though, he planned to put his sadness on hold and enjoy the rest of the day with Sierra.

"DO YOU ACCEPT the challenge?" Ben's loud, dramatic voice rose above the whirring, beeping video machines

that made the Indigo Springs Arcade a popular afternoon hangout.

"Considering you dragged me here by calling me
a chicken in short shorts," Sierra said, "I don't see I
have a choice."

"You don't," he agreed cheerfully.

She gazed down at the undersized basketball she
held, which looked to be about the size of the rims
attached to two horizontal hoops. The object of the
game was to sink more shots than your opponent.

"Then let's do it," Sierra said.

He pressed a button, switching on a mechanical
voice that counted down from three. As soon as the
voice gave the prompt, Sierra let her basketball fly. It
swooshed through the hoop while Ben's rimmed out.
A score of 1-0 appear in red neon letters above the
hoops.

Beginner's luck, Sierra thought. She grabbed for
another ball and shot again. Another basket! Adrenaline coursed through her.

"Swish!" someone yelled. She was surprised to
realize she was that someone.

"The battle's just beginning," Ben cried out.

They fired basketballs at the hoop with frenzied
abandon, with Sierra's shock at her rate of success
rivaled only by the joy of her laughter.

She couldn't help herself. It was just so much darn
fun. The artificial voice signaled time was running out.
Sierra managed to fling up four more basketballs, three
of which hit the mark.

A shrill buzzer sounded. Holding her breath, she

checked the final score. It wasn't even close. She'd won by a two-to-one margin.

She raised her arms in the air, whooped and did a little dance. Ben grinned.

"Enjoyed that, did you?" He didn't say he'd told her she would, not that she would have minded. The novelty of victory was too thrilling. "You didn't tell me you were a ringer."

"I've never played this game before in my life!"

"Don't ask if I was on my high school basketball team," he said, "because I won't answer on the grounds that it may embarrass me."

"Don't worry. I won't make you wave a white flag." She edged closer to him so their bodies touched, then spoke into his ear. "That would be letting you off too easily. I'll think of another way for you to pay up."

"I should lose more often," he said.

A delicious shiver traveled the length of her body. For what seemed like the hundredth time, she reassured herself she was doing the right thing by not telling him her father was in town when his mother died.

What purpose would it serve other than to needlessly raise his suspicions? She knew in her heart—no, in her very soul—her father was blameless in Allison Blaine's death.

If he hadn't already, Ben was very close to reaching the inevitable conclusion his mother had died exactly the way he'd been told. In an accident. It would be cruel, especially on the eve of his mother's birthday, to tell him anything that might cause him to keep probing into the incident.

"How about I make you dinner?" he asked.

"You can cook?"

"It's one of my many talents." He exaggerated a suggestive voice. "Let's get out of here and you can start sampling them."

She was laughing when he took her hand and led her toward the exit. The place was populated mostly by teenagers, but parents stood by as much younger children played skeet ball and some of the simpler games.

A boy about four years old dashed onto the sidewalk when Ben held the front door of the arcade open for Sierra.

"Nathan! No!" a woman cried.

Ben was through the door in an instant, bending over and swooping up the boy. Judging by the little guy's still-churning legs, he hadn't seen the interception coming. He was a cutie, even with his flushed cheeks and hairline damp with sweat.

"Where you going in such a hurry, buddy?" Ben asked.

"I scream!" the boy yelled.

He had that right, Sierra thought.

"I scream," the boy repeated, pointing to a white truck with a large sliding window traveling down Main Street. The vehicle was brightly decorated with images of Popsicles, sodas and, lastly, ice cream. Its jingle was off, signaling the driver had called it quits for the day.

A skinny woman with frizzy blond hair wearing baggy madras capris burst out of the arcade. It was Edie Clark, who'd been in Sierra's graduating class at Indigo Springs High.

"Thank God you caught him before he ran into the

street." Edie practically sagged with relief. "I can't thank you enough."

A second boy appeared from behind Edie, heading rapidly in the same direction as the first.

"No, Jason!" Edie warned.

Little Jason kept running. With a deft move, Ben caught the second boy and lifted him so he held both brothers. The boys were identical, from their mops of brown hair to their Thomas the Tank Engine T-shirts to their petulant expressions.

"Ice cream! Ice cream!" the twins chanted even as the truck moved farther down the street.

"No. No ice cream. It's almost time for dinner." Edie, her face pinched with strain, took Jason from Ben. She set him down, keeping a firm hold on his hand.

"Want ice cream!" Nathan shouted, thrusting his small body this way and that in an attempt to escape Ben's arms.

"Stop yelling!" Edie yelled.

"Hey, Nathan, what's that behind Jason's ear?" Ben asked in a loud voice. He reached out and pulled out a quarter. Nathan's mouth opened, then he grinned.

"I think I see another quarter behind Nathan's ear." Ben set Nathan down beside his brother, repeated the sequence and produced another coin. Nathan giggled. Jason clapped his chubby hands before Edie grabbed one of them.

"Whoever you are," Edie said to Ben, "I owe you my life."

Ben laughed and introduced himself, omitting his affiliation with the *Pittsburgh Tribune*. Edie started to say something, but then both boys tugged on her hands at once. She traveled a good three steps before she got them under control.

"It's time I got these boys home." Edie looked pointedly at Sierra. "You've got a good man there, Sierra. Don't let him get away."

Edie couldn't hold back her fidgety twins any longer. The three of them headed down the sidewalk, taking Sierra's chance to correct Edie's misconception with them.

Sierra watched her former classmate retreat. "That's not good. Edie likes to talk. She'll tell everyone we're involved."

"Isn't that what Friday night was all about?" he asked.

Friday night had been about proving she could be wild and unpredictable with an unsuitable man. If Edie spread it around that Ben was good with kids, it would sound like Ben was relationship material.

"How did you know how to handle Edie's twins anyway?" She sidestepped the question and resumed walking in the direction of the downtown grocery.

"I tried the coin trick on my brother's kid the last time I saw him," he said. "Turns out distraction works."

"How old is your nephew?"

"Two or three, I think," he said. "Or maybe four. I'm not real sure."

"When was the last time you saw him?"

"It's been a while," Ben answered vaguely.

They slowed to pass a couple who'd stopped to

admire a painting of a landscape in an art gallery window. Ben took hold of her hand as they filed past. When she returned her gaze to the sidewalk, she spotted Chad Armstrong exiting her favorite Thai restaurant carrying a brown paper bag.

Her step faltered as the day of the week registered. Chad always got takeout Thai on Tuesdays before spending an hour at the Blue Haven.

"What's wrong?" Ben asked, then followed her gaze. "Oh, I see."

She doubted he could when she didn't have a clear view of the situation herself. Chad was upon them in seconds, his lips pursed, the way he held them in disapproval.

"Sierra." His expression softened when he looked at her, then tightened when he nodded to Ben. "Nash."

"Armstrong," Ben said with an answering nod. They regarded each other warily, like prize fighters facing off in the ring.

"The food smells good," Sierra said, mostly to break the uneasy silence.

Chad held up the paper bag. "It's the pad thai."

Her favorite.

"Will you be at the committee meeting Thursday?" he asked.

He must know the answer since it was the last meeting before the festival got underway on Friday.

"Yes," she confirmed.

"Good. I need to speak with you about something." He dipped his head, then was gone.

"I get the impression he doesn't like me," Ben said.

"He's not real fond of me, either," Sierra said.

"I don't know about that." At some point Ben had let go of her. He shoved his hands into his pockets. "My guess is he wants to talk to you about getting back together."

If that were true, would she take Chad back? A month ago—no, even a few days ago—the decision would have been easy. She'd have put aside her hurt feelings and been relieved her future was back on track.

But now…now everything had changed.

They resumed walking toward the grocery store in silence.

"It's okay if we call it a night," Ben said. "I don't have to make you dinner."

She could end things between them right now. Today had been an aberration, a window in time where they played at being in a relationship. Very soon he'd be gone.

"You don't have to stay with me tonight, either," she said slowly, "but I'd really like it if you did."

He stopped, turned and gazed into her eyes. "Are you sure?"

"Very sure."

"In that case," he said, "I'm going to make you one hell of a delicious dinner."

It was the perfect thing to say. She laughed, the mood instantly lightening.

Good thing he was leaving soon, Sierra thought. Because if he stayed much longer, her heart would be in serious trouble.

CHAPTER NINE

THE ROLLING STONES yanked Ben out of a deep sleep.

It was his cell phone, playing a riff about getting no satisfaction. That certainly hadn't been the case last night, he thought languorously. He and Sierra had ended up in bed before the ingredients for the seafood pasta were out of the grocery bag. Dessert, much later in the evening, had been another bout of lovemaking.

He opened his eyes, and Sierra's bedroom came into focus. He'd fallen asleep with her snuggled against him, the naked skin of her back nestled against his front, her head tucked under his chin. Now her side of the bed was empty, the sheets cold to the touch.

His cell phone was no longer singing. He'd received a text, not a call.

He found his phone in the pocket of his blue jeans on the floor next to the bed and clicked through until he got to the message. It was from Joe Geraldi, his boss.

I need you on the group home story, it read. *Now.*

He deleted the text. He'd answer it later, hopefully after he made progress on his mother's story and could justify his continued stay in Indigo Springs.

Even with the shades drawn, the room wasn't fully

dark. He knew from his cell phone that it was nearly eight. He was amazed he'd slept so heavily considering his mother's birthday had dawned. He typically got little rest when the date was imminent.

He got out of bed and deliberately turned his mind to Sierra. He couldn't hear *SportsCenter* playing on the television. Where was she? The note he found on the kitchen table answered his question.

Went into work, she'd written. *If you head back to Pittsburgh today, please know you made* temporary *my favorite word.*

Disappointment sliced through him, as sharp as a razor blade. He searched his memory, failing to understand why she thought he might be leaving today. He was certain he hadn't told her that.

His hand inadvertently hit a stack of papers on the kitchen counter, knocking half of them to the floor.

"Damn," he cursed softly.

He stooped down, gathering a magazine, a couple of envelopes, some advertising flyers and assorted pieces of paper. The last item he picked up was a photo.

He started to put the photo back on the stack with the other papers when he saw it was a picture of Sierra's brother. Except on closer inspection, he realized it wasn't Ryan. The man, who wore an orange hat and held a golf club, only looked like Ryan. That must mean the man was Dr. Whitmore.

He turned the photo over, confirming his guess. *Ryan at the Lakeview Pines golf tournament,* somebody had scribbled. He remembered seeing an advertisement for the resort when he was en route to Indigo Springs.

There was another line of printing on the back of the photo. A date. He blinked, squinting to make sure he'd read correctly.

The photo had been taken the day his mother died.

Feeling like he was operating on autopilot, he returned the photo to the middle of the stack of papers and let himself out of the town house.

Beads of sweat had broken out on his forehead by the time he reached the street. A cool breeze carrying the scent of spring blossoms blew over his face, chilling him.

Whoever sent that e-mail incriminating Dr. Whitmore must have known something. Why else had Rosemary Whitmore lied about her husband being out of town when Ben's mother died?

Mrs. Whitmore obviously knew more than she was telling.

He drew a ragged breath that hurt his chest. Considering where he'd found the photo, so, too, did Sierra.

"WELL, WHAT DO YOU THINK?"

Sara Brenneman emerged from the dressing room at the Harrisburg bridal shop late on Wednesday afternoon, almost completely engulfed by a wedding gown with huge puffed sleeves, a frilly neckline and a full-skirted ball gown of silk taffeta.

She twirled around. Sierra sucked in a breath, afraid the bride-to-be's feet would get tangled in the cathedral-length train. If she toppled while wearing that dress, she might never get herself upright.

"I think you look like the Stay Puft Marshmallow

Woman," Annie Sublinski Whitmore said. Sierra's sister-in-law was sitting next to Sierra in the area the shop had set aside for the friends and family members who were on hand to give helpful advice. "What possessed you to try that one on, anyway?"

"I already told you. This is the gown most like the one Princess Di wore." She balled her hands into fists and balanced them on the layers of taffeta that sprung out from the waistline of the gown. "What do you think, Sierra?"

Sierra bit her lip before she said she suspected the gown could stand on its own even without someone inside. "I think it's a little poofier than the one Princess Di wore."

The bride-to-be examined herself in the bank of mirrors that ran the full length of the back wall of the shop. Besides showing a woman in a voluminous gown, the reflection revealed her mischievous expression.

"Sara Brenneman, you're playing with us!" Annie exclaimed. "You know you look like a marshmallow!"

"Of course I know. I'm not blind," Sara said, giggling. "I should buy it. If Michael married me when I looked like this, I'd know he really loved me."

"You already know that," Annie said. "Now go change out of that thing. You're hurting my eyes."

They could still hear Sara's laughter after she disappeared back inside the dressing room, where the shop assistant waited to help her out of the gown.

"Please tell me I wasn't that much trouble when we went shopping for my wedding dress," Annie said.

"You?" Sierra raised her eyebrows. "Hardly. You bought the first dress you tried on."

"That's because I didn't have the Princess Di wedding fantasy," Annie said.

"I thought it was because you have an aversion to shopping," Sierra teased.

Annie made a face at her. "I like to think I'm a smart shopper. Not only did I have the sense to bring along an authority, I listened to her."

"I'm hardly an expert," Sierra said.

"Maybe not, but you're really good at picking out what looks best," Annie said. "I can't tell you how glad I am—and how glad Sara will be—that you came along today. I know how busy you are."

The three women had set out for Harrisburg and the Extravagance bridal boutique as soon as Sierra finished with her last patient. Laurie Grieb was supposed to come along, but she canceled at the last minute because she wasn't feeling well.

The owner of Extravagance, a woman Sierra had known in college, had already left for the day. Her assistant, who was juggling her time between customers, reported she had orders to take very good care of them.

"I'm not that busy," Sierra denied.

"That's right. You did take the day off yesterday because of that hot guy you're seeing."

Sierra fought the dejection that had threatened to overwhelm her since she'd left Ben Nash sleeping in her bed that morning. At any other time in her life, she'd consider herself in a relationship after making love with a man. Not this time. Not when she hadn't heard from the man in question all day and he could be back in Pittsburgh by now.

"I'm not seeing anyone," Sierra denied.

"That's not what Ryan told me," Annie said. "He said Ben Nash called to ask if you could skip work."

Sierra could hardly dispute that.

A slight rustling followed by footsteps coming from the direction of the dressing room interrupted them. Saved by the bride-to-be, Sierra thought.

Sara appeared wearing a strapless satin A-line gown with an embroidered bodice that Sierra had suggested she try on. The slim skirt was two-tiered, part of it swept up at the side and held in place by a jeweled broach. "How about this one?" she asked.

"It's gorgeous!" Annie jumped up from her chair and went to her friend's side, standing back slightly to stare at her. "Just stunning."

"It does look good." Sara ran a hand down the satiny material of the dress, which clung to her torso then flared slightly, creating a swirling effect.

"Good? That's like saying van Gogh's paintings were okay. I told you Sierra would know what looked good on you!"

"It's not that difficult when Sara's trying on the gowns. Just about anything would look good on her." Sierra paused. "Except that first gown."

"Forget about the poofy dress. This is the one!" Annie declared, seeming to have forgotten her aversion to shopping. "She looks like a vision in white. Doesn't she look like a vision in white, Sierra?"

"A white vision," Sierra agreed, crossing her legs

and sitting back in her chair. Now that they were no longer talking about Ben Nash, she might be able to put him out of her mind. She'd have to sooner or later, considering she might never see him again. She swallowed the lump in her throat and focused on wedding fashion. "A pair of white high-heeled satin pumps, the simpler the better, would be perfect with that dress."

"You can wear your hair in one of those fancy sweep-ups," Annie suggested.

"You mean updos," Sierra corrected gently.

"Yes." Annie didn't take offense. "Maybe a couple of little flowers but no veil."

Sara gazed at herself in the mirror, as though picturing herself on the momentous day. "I don't know," she said slowly. "There's something about the dress that's not quite right." She wrinkled her nose. "I don't think I like white."

Of course. The lawyer favored bold colors and flashy prints in her everyday wardrobe. Sierra should have taken that into consideration.

"I have an idea." Putting Ben Nash firmly out of her mind, Sierra moved through the shop, locating the area where they'd found the strapless gown. Like most bridal shops, Extravagance kept a limited number of samples in the store, strongly suggesting its customers have gowns made to order. Luckily the sample Sierra wanted was available in the right size. She hurried back to her friends and held it up.

"It's the same dress in gold!" Sara declared. "I love that."

"I told you Sierra knew fashion," Annie said.

Sara took the dress from Sierra and clutched it to her bosom. "I know this is the one. How can I thank you, Sierra? Wait. I know. Michael and I will treat you and Ben to dinner!"

Sierra tensed, shoring up her defenses. She hadn't awakened Ben that morning because she was practicing distancing her emotions for when he left town. Since he'd neither stopped by the office nor called, maybe he was already gone. It made sense that he wouldn't want to spend his mother's birthday in the town where she'd died.

"Ben and I aren't dating," Sierra said, repeating the same information she'd relayed to her sister-in-law.

"Really?" The bride-to-be wrinkled her nose. "That's not what I hear."

"You like him, right?" The question came from Annie.

Sierra had learned how to expertly evade questions that were too personal. With Annie and Sara regarding her with concern, as well as interest, she found to her surprise that she wanted to answer.

"Yes, I like him," Sierra admitted. "I like him a lot."

"Then what's to stop you from dating him?" Annie asked. "He's obviously into you."

"He lives in Pittsburgh. I live in Indigo Springs."

"He's in Indigo Springs now," Annie pointed out.

"I'm not sure he is." Sierra wasn't prepared for the rush of sadness that hit her. "He's about wrapped up his business in town."

"No, he hasn't." Sara shook her head decisively. "He's working on a story about some tourist who fell from the overlook years ago, right?"

"How do you know that?" Sierra asked. An inane question. Everybody in town probably was aware of his purpose by now.

"When I went into Jimmy's Diner for coffee this morning, I saw him having a late breakfast with Quincy Coleman," she said. "He was asking about the tourist."

"How do you know what they were talking about?"

"I had to wait for the coffee," she said. "They were only sitting a few seats away from me at the counter."

"Did you hear anything else they said?" Sierra asked.

"Only bits and pieces. I wasn't really listening. Oh. But I did hear Ben ask about your father." She winked. "That sounds to me like a man who's interested in you."

Sierra suddenly found it difficult to draw breath. Just days ago Ben had promised not to grill the towns-people about her father. He'd gone back on his word.

"I can't wait to try this on," Sara said, cradling the gold gown.

"I'll help," Annie said.

The two of them disappeared into the dressing room. Sierra didn't move, but her world tilted on an axis. Un-easiness roiled inside her. Last night she could have sworn Ben had given up his quest to sully her father's name. That no longer seemed to be the case.

It was looking increasingly likely she'd slept with the enemy.

DUSK SETTLED OVER the mountain, muting the view from the overlook. The trees blended together in a dark green blur, and the Lehigh River below was impossible to see.

Ben stood with his hands resting on the waist-high railing that ran along the lip of the mountain ledge. He was, unsurprisingly, alone.

The Riverview Overlook would be busiest when the sun was high in the sky, bathing the valley in light. It probably also got a fair amount of traffic at night from teenagers scouting for a dark place to make out.

At twilight, however, there was little reason to be here. Yet this was the time of day his mother had died. According to Alex Rawlings, his grandparents reported his mother liked to come up here to think. Was that what she'd been doing? If not, had she been alone?

He leaned forward, squinting down the side of the mountain. Visibility was poor, but he could still tell the ground dropped steeply.

Because of the vagaries of erosion, there was no way to tell for sure what the terrain had been like nineteen years ago. If the town hadn't erected a railing until after her death, how bad could it have been?

Treacherous enough that his mother had plunged to her death. If, that is, she fell. He still couldn't accept that scenario, even though he'd only been able to find circumstantial evidence to the contrary.

The anonymous e-mail pointing to Dr. Whitmore. The lie Mrs. Whitmore told about her husband's whereabouts at the time of the death. Sierra's failure to alert him her mother had lied.

The last one stung far more than it should have. Almost as disappointing as his failure to make progress on the story was his eagerness to let himself become distracted. By a Whitmore, no less.

"I'm sorry I'm not getting anywhere, Mom," he said aloud, except she couldn't hear him. Nobody could.

A sound rang out in the silence. His body jerked and his heart jumped before his brain belatedly relayed the source.

His cell phone.

Feeling like a fool, he took the phone from his pocket and checked the illuminated small screen. It showed an unfamiliar number with a Philadelphia area code. After a moment's hesitation, he established the connection.

"Hello," he said.

"Ben. It's Connor." His younger brother. "I'm glad I finally reached you. The cell number I had for you was wrong."

Ben had changed his when the newspaper issued its reporters new phones earlier in the year.

He yanked himself out of the past and focused on his brother. When had he seen him last? Christmas, he thought. "How have you been, Connor?"

"Good. I got promoted to assistant manager at work." Ben blanked for a moment before recalling his brother had a job in the sales division of a computer hardware company.

"Congratulations," Ben said. "How about Sally and the kids? How are they?"

"Growing like weeds. The kids. Not Sally. But I didn't call to talk about me." He paused. "I wanted to see how you were doing."

Ben peered out over the railing. His brother had remembered her birthday, too. "I'm fine."

"Your office told me how to get in touch with you." Connor's words were measured. "They also told me you were in Indigo Springs working on a story. Is it about Mom?"

Ben didn't see any reason not to fill his brother in. "Yeah."

He relayed information about the e-mail that started the whole thing, ending with the leads he'd followed today. It had been easy to confirm Dr. Whitmore had played in the Lakeview Pines golf tournament the year his mother died. He'd been less successful getting back in touch with Mrs. Whitmore. He'd driven to Mountain Village Estates when she didn't answer her phone, but the gatekeeper claimed she wasn't home.

Ben didn't mention the fruitless conversation he'd had that morning with Quincy Coleman, who didn't remember his mother ever stepping foot in the bank.

Neither did he mention Sierra and the information she'd withheld.

"It's been frustrating," Ben said. A colossal understatement. "I know in my gut there's something to this, but I can't find it."

"It was a long time ago," Connor said. "It's tough for some people to remember what happened last week, let alone nineteen years ago."

"How about you?" Ben asked. "You were here in Indigo Springs when she died."

"I was four years old," Connor said. "My mind's pretty much a blank. All I remember about Mom is one day she was here and the next she was gone."

Ben had wandered away from the railing as he and his brother talked. Next to him was a bench strategically positioned to take advantage of the view. He sank into it, feeling profoundly sad. "That's all you remember about her?"

"Not quite," Connor said. "You know that scar on my temple? Sometimes when I notice it in the mirror, I can see her clear as day. I was horsing around like usual, tripped and fell into the edge of a table. Then there she was, smoothing back my hair, kissing my forehead, whispering soothing words. I always think of that when I think of her."

Ben's throat felt so full, all he could do was nod. His memories of their mother, although more numerous, were along the same vein.

Connor restarted the conversation, asking where in town Ben was staying. Ben told him about securing a room despite the tourists who'd started to fill up the town. They spent a few more minutes talking about nothing in particular until they ran out of things to say.

"Take care of yourself, man," Connor said. "Keep in touch."

Ben disconnected the call and wiped away what felt suspiciously like a tear. All these years, he believed he was the one most affected by his mother's death. Connor's phone call taught him that wasn't necessarily true.

He should take comfort that there was someone else in his corner. Sitting in the darkness at the place she'd died, he no longer felt he was seeking answers only for himself. He was responsible for finding them for Connor, too.

A LONE CAR OCCUPIED one of the few parking spaces at the Riverview Overlook. Darkness had settled like thick, black fog over Indigo Springs, which would have made it difficult to distinguish the make and model if the car wasn't silver.

She'd spotted Ben's car at the overlook on the drive back from Harrisburg, but hadn't pointed it out to Sara and Annie. As soon as they dropped her off, she'd gotten into her own car and went to confront him.

She swung her Lexus into the parking lot alongside his Sebring, immediately verifying the driver's seat was empty. Before she switched off the ignition, her headlights illuminated a lone man sitting on the bench, facing the valley with his back toward her.

Ben.

Even with fifteen feet separating them, she could feel his hands running over her skin, his mouth moving on hers, his body joining with her.

His betrayal.

She gathered her composure, got out of the car and approached the bench. Wordlessly she sat down beside him. Only then did he turn.

"Hello, Sierra," he said.

She dipped her head. "Ben."

Since discovering he'd questioned Quincy Coleman about her father, she'd intended to take him to task, asking how dare he renew his efforts to incriminate her father when he had no evidence of wrongdoing.

How dare he make love to her and then deceive her.

Yet here, at the place where his mother had died, on

his mother's birthday, she didn't have the heart. So she said nothing.

He seemed content to sit in silence. They'd been as close as two people could be the night before—as intimate as Sierra had ever been with anyone—yet they didn't touch. The dozen or so inches between them could have been twelve miles.

The seconds passed, time seeming inconsequential on the mountain. She smelled evergreen and fresh, cool air. The rustling she heard could have been the wind blowing through the leaves on the trees or the nocturnal wildlife moving from place to place.

"I got your note this morning." When he spoke, his voice sounded unnaturally loud. "I was surprised you thought I might leave town."

It was a logical assumption. Despite his probing, he'd turned up nothing. Even the managing editor of his newspaper agreed. "You said your boss wants you back in Pittsburgh."

"I didn't say I was going. Someone sent me that e-mail. Like I told you, I won't leave until I find out who." His flinty tone brought home how badly she'd misjudged his obstinacy. He was like a dog with an old bone he wouldn't let go.

"That doesn't explain why you were questioning Quincy Coleman about my father this morning," she said. "Don't look so surprised. I have sources, too. I know you went back on your word."

"My word? You're one to talk." He turned his head sharply. The sky was overcast with the few stars present providing almost no visibility. She still felt like his stare cut into her. "I know you lied to me."

She stopped breathing.

"This morning at your place I knocked over some papers in the kitchen by accident." He spoke without inflection. "When I picked them up, I came across a photo of your father in an orange golf hat."

She didn't have to ask if he'd realized the significance of the writing on the back of the photo.

"I never lied to you," Sierra said.

"Oh, really?" he asked sarcastically. "You didn't correct your mother when she insisted your whole family was out of town when my mom died."

"That's not the way it was," she denied. "I didn't find the photo until later."

"So only your mother lied?"

"She didn't." Sierra resurrected the rationale she'd used with her brother. "It slipped her mind that there was one year we didn't vacation the first week in July."

"How do you know that?" he asked. "Did she tell you?"

Sierra hadn't talked to her mother since coming across the photo. Rosemary Whitmore had taken a bus trip to Atlantic City with some friends from the Mountain Village Estates. She seldom turned on her cell phone. Sierra wasn't even sure her mother knew how to check for missed calls.

"Don't bother to answer," he said. "I can tell by your silence that she didn't."

"Only because I haven't been able to reach her," Sierra retorted.

"Tell you what," he said. "Let's talk to her together. I think she could be the key."

"The key to what?" she asked. "You've been in town long enough to know what kind of man my father was. Do you honestly believe he killed your mother?"

"I don't know what to believe," he said.

"I'm sorry about your mother. I really am. But it's ridiculous to even consider my father had anything to do with her death," she said. "You don't have a shred of evidence. An anonymous e-mail doesn't count."

"If it's so ridiculous, let's go see your mother and clear it up right now," he said.

"My mother's out of town."

"*Conveniently* out of town." He didn't pause for breath, continuing before she could argue. "When will she be back home?"

"I don't know," Sierra said.

Her eyes had adjusted enough to the darkness that she picked up the lift of his eyebrows. She kept her expression neutral so he wouldn't continue to press her. Rosemary Whitmore planned to spend the festival weekend with Ryan and Annie when she returned from Atlantic City. Ben might be gone by then.

Ben rose from the bench. She could barely make out more than his silhouette in the darkness.

"Let me ask you something, Sierra," Ben said. "If you're so sure your father is blameless, why did you just lie to me again?"

He didn't wait for an answer, turning and walking to his car.

She couldn't have given him one, anyway.

CHAPTER TEN

THE LOBBY OF THE Indigo Inn, the venerable hotel that had served the town for three decades, was deserted shortly before eight on Thursday morning except for the graying, middle-aged man waiting at the front desk.

Sierra hung back, glad for a few more minutes to compose herself. Her palms were sweating, her stomach was jumping, and she was fighting the urge to rush for the exit.

That would be the coward's way out, exactly the route she refused to let herself take. What she had to tell Ben should be said face-to-face, even if it meant she'd be late for work.

The man in front of Sierra slanted her a weary smile. With his blocky build and slight paunch, he looked neither like an art lover in town for the festival nor an outdoorsman. The dark smudges under his eyes and his rumpled clothing made it appear as though he'd gotten even less sleep than she had.

"The guy who works here will be back soon," the man said. "Some guest lost his key."

"Thanks," Sierra said. Considering the size of the

crowd the town was expecting for this weekend's festival, she hoped he'd thought ahead to make a reservation.

A short, thin man wearing a suit jacket and sporting a wispy moustache hurried across the carpeted lobby with quick steps and let himself around the desk. Sierra recognized the desk clerk from the times she'd seen him bustling around town.

"Sorry about that." The clerk gave the stranger a bright smile. He either mainlined caffeine or he was a morning person. "Now what can I do you for?"

"I need Ben Nash's room number."

Sierra's senses went on alert, the fatigue leaving her in an instant.

"I'm not permitted to give out room numbers, but I can certainly ring his room for you," the clerk said in his chirpy voice. "Who shall I tell him is calling?"

"His father," the stranger said.

His father! Sierra wouldn't have figured out the connection on her own. The man looked nothing like tall, lean Ben, who she recalled resembled his mother.

The clerk picked up the phone and punched in some numbers. After what must have been several rings, he relayed the message, then hung up. His face contorted, his teeth flashing as he gritted them. "It's room six, but before you go I should warn you that I may have woken him up. He sounds a little grumpy."

"Thanks for the heads-up." Ben's father didn't seem unduly concerned as he headed away from the front desk in the direction of the first-floor guest rooms.

Sierra ignored the clerk's welcoming smile and

followed Ben's father, catching up to him in the hallway adjacent to the elevator.

"Mr. Nash!" she called. "Wait."

His steps faltered, and he turned. His features were
coarser than Ben's, but he had the same strong jawline.
"Sorry. Do I know you?"

"My name's Sierra Whitmore." She half expected
him to react to the surname, but it didn't appear to
mean anything to him. "I heard you tell the clerk who
you are. I'm here to see your son, too."

His bewilderment turned to curiosity. "He expecting you?"

"No," she said.

"Me, neither." Ben's father seemed to be a man of
few words. "How do you know my son?"

She might as well tell him. He'd been married to
Allison Blaine. He'd loved her. He'd be as affected by
news of her as Ben. "My father is the man who was
mentioned in the e-mail."

"You mean that e-mail Ben got at the newspaper?
His brother mentioned something about that." He
sounded as if he was fuzzy on the facts.

"It's why Ben's in town." She decided on full disclosure, no matter how difficult. "The e-mail implicated
my father in your wife's death."

"What?" Mr. Nash screwed up his face. "Your father
had nothing to do with that."

Her heartbeat accelerated at his unexpected an-
nouncement. She moved a step closer to him. "My
father's name was Dr. Ryan Whitmore. Did you know
him?"

"Never heard of him."

A door at the end of the hall opened, then closed. A barefoot woman carrying an ice bucket disappeared into a nook. A sound like thunder, which was more likely the clanking of ice cubes dropping into the container, matched the frantic pounding of Sierra's heart.

"Then why did you say my father wasn't involved?" Sierra asked with an urgency she couldn't disguise. "I know he was innocent, but how do you?"

"Ah, hell. Ben's been hassling your family about this, hasn't he?"

"Yes," Sierra admitted.

"I was afraid of that." Ben's father's face contorted into a mask of misery. "It's my fault for not setting that son of mine straight a long time ago."

The hammering of Sierra's heart increased. "Set him straight about what?"

"About what really happened to his mother. That's what I'm here to tell him."

BEN SAT ON THE EDGE of his unmade bed, rubbing the sleep from his eyes. Sierra came into focus, wearing a pale yellow blouse showing a hint of cleavage and a skirt baring her lovely calves. With tendrils of brown hair escaping from her upswept hair, she looked more like the woman he'd made love to than a doctor.

His gaze shifted slightly to the left of Sierra, who was positioned in the chair beside the hotel-room desk.

Occupying an armchair in the corner of the room was his father, his heavy eyebrows forming an inverted

V, the lines around his mouth and eyes more pronounced than when Ben had seen him last.

While Ben's subconscious might conjure up Sierra in his hotel room, no way would it add his father.

Unfortunately, that meant he wasn't dreaming.

"Do either of you want to tell me what you're doing here?" Ben wasn't sure which of the two he'd been more surprised to find at his hotel-room door. Probably his father. He hadn't seen or talked to him in months.

"I ran into this young lady in the lobby." His father had always been an expert at avoiding the direct question, leaving Ben to draw his own conclusions. He guessed Connor had told their father where to find Ben, but couldn't fathom why his old man had felt compelled to make the two-hour drive from Philadelphia.

"I overheard him tell the desk clerk he was your father." Sierra's response wasn't any more enlightening. When her chest expanded, as though she was fortifying herself with oxygen, he realized she wasn't through talking. "I'm here to apologize."

Ben said nothing. Her refusal to be straight with him last night had hurt, and he was unwilling to make things easier for her.

"You were right. I do know where my mother is." Her words were slow and measured. "She's in Atlantic City with a group from her retirement community. She's bad about answering her cell phone so it wouldn't do any good to call her. But she'll be in town for the festival."

"Last night you were determined to keep me away from your mother," Ben said. "Why the change of heart?"

"You were right. Why should I lie when there's nothing to hide?" Her eyes touched on his, the look in them contrite. "I'm sorry, Ben. I never should have lied to you in the first place."

As easily as that, he forgave her.

"I'm missing something." Deep furrows appeared in his father's brow. "I don't get why you need to talk to the doctor's wife, Ben. It's not about that e-mail, is it?"

"In a way." Ben avoided looking at Sierra. "I haven't been able to rule out Dr. Whitmore's involvement in Mom's death."

"I don't care what that e-mail said," his father stated forcefully. "That doctor had nothing to do with it."

In the past whenever Ben had asked for details about his mother's death, he'd received a neutral response before his father changed the subject. Ben had never pressed the issue, figuring his father had no more information to share.

"How can you be sure of that?" Ben asked. "You were across the state when she died."

"There are things about your mom you don't know." His father's head sagged, as though he was having trouble holding it up. "Things I should have told you a long time ago."

"What things?"

His father looked pointedly at Sierra, then back at him. "This isn't something you'll be wanting an audience to hear."

Sierra instantly got to her feet. "You're right. I'll leave you two alone."

It made sense for her to go. If his father revealed

anything Sierra needed to know, Ben could fill her in later. She touched him on the arm, silently conveying with a look that she was on his side.

Before he realized he was going to reach for it, he caught her hand. It felt like an anchor. She gazed at him questioningly with the same expression that had softened him earlier. "I'd like for you to stay," he said.

"You sure?" The question came from his father, whose eyes darted between them. If he were trying to figure out the nature of their relationship, it was an impossible task. "This is gonna be hard for you to hear, Ben. That's why I drove up here to tell you in person."

"I'm sure," Ben said. "But it's up to Sierra."

He let go of her hand so she wouldn't feel pressured to stay if she was disinclined. Sierra sat down on the bed beside him without another word.

His father closed his eyes and kneaded the space above his nose for a good five seconds before he started to talk. "Your mom didn't come to Indigo Springs to visit her parents, son. She came to live with them. She wanted a divorce."

Ben's stomach churned and beads of sweat popped up on his forehead. The possibility of trouble in his parents' marriage had occurred to him when he heard about her trip to the bank, but he'd discounted it.

"Me and your mother, we had problems. Right from the start," his father continued. "She wasn't even eighteen when you were born. Way too young to be a mom."

"She was a good mother." Ben could hear the defensiveness in his voice, even as he recognized the rocky beginning could explain why his mother had kept her maiden name.

"Yeah, she was," his father said. "Should have said she was too young to be married. She tried to make it work, but it was hard. I was on the road, driving my truck, working my butt off to make a living. She was at home by herself, watching all three of you kids. I didn't even notice her getting depressed."

"Depressed?" Ben repeated. "That doesn't sound like Mom."

"She did a good job hiding it. Don't think you ever saw her crying." He shook his head. "I couldn't understand what was wrong with her. When I got off the road, I needed downtime. But she said caring for you boys was too much for her. She kept taking off, leaving me with you kids. Then I'd find out somebody had seen her in the neighborhood, just sitting in her car."

The information was coming so fast Ben could hardly process it. He'd been twelve when his mother died, but surely that was old enough to figure out something was wrong. He hadn't sensed a thing.

"Did she see a doctor about her condition?" Sierra interjected.

"Not then," his father answered. "That was mostly my fault. I told her to snap out of it. But things just kept getting worse. She wasn't eating. Some days she could hardly get out of bed."

His father paused, and Ben was struck with a dim memory of himself banging through the door and calling for his mother after coming home to a silent house. An image crystallized of her in bed with the covers pulled up to her chin. She'd said she was sick, that a neighbor was watching his brothers.

"Then one day she told me…" His father stopped and cleared his throat before starting again. "She told me she'd thought about killing herself."

Ben shook his head despite the memory of his mother in bed in the middle of the day. His father seemed to be talking about a stranger. "No," he said. "Mom loved us. She wouldn't have done that."

"You didn't let me finish, son. It scared her bad. Scared me, too. That's when I wised up about her seeing a doctor."

"Dr. Whitmore?" Ben asked.

"No. A doctor back home. He put her on something. An antidepressant." He named the brand. "Then she was like her old self. But things didn't go back to normal."

"What do you mean?" Ben asked.

"She started nagging me to find another job so I could be home more." His father massaged the back of his neck, as though the story was causing him pain. "I couldn't do that. Not with a mortgage, a wife and three kids to feed. I never thought she'd up and leave me."

It was a sad story, but hardly a tragic one. If that was all there was to it, his parents would have divorced and Ben and his brothers would have spent the rest of their childhood in Indigo Springs.

His father drew a deep breath. "At some point, she must have stopped taking her antidepressants. After she died, her blood sample came back clean. No trace of drugs in her system at all."

Ben wanted to tell his father to shut up, but he couldn't find his voice. Sierra put her hand on his thigh and lightly squeezed, as though bracing him for his father's next words.

"Son, I'm pretty sure your mother didn't fall from that cliff," he said. "I think she jumped."

BEN SAT WITH SIERRA in a quiet corner of Jimmy's Diner, where they'd gone after his father headed back to Philadelphia. He wasn't hungry, but she'd insisted he needed to fortify himself with breakfast.

Food wouldn't help him deal with the feelings roiling inside him. At this point, he didn't think anything would. Except, possibly, Sierra. She was the sole bright point in what was turning out to be a dismal morning.

"Your apology meant a lot to me," Ben said after he placed his order with Ellie Marson, their waitress. "It's ironic that now I owe you one."

"You owe me nothing," Sierra said. "Everything you did was because you loved your mother, the same way I loved my father."

"Yeah, I loved her." He couldn't keep bitterness from spilling over into his words. "Turns out it was a hell of a lot more than she loved me and my brothers."

Sierra's eyes widened. "Why would you say something like that?"

"You heard my father. She got off her antidepressants. If she loved us so much, why did she do that? Why just give up?"

"You don't know that she gave up." Sierra anchored

her forearms on the table and leaned forward. "She might have gotten off the medication because she was suffering from side effects. The right antidepressant can work miracles. The wrong one can be a disaster."

He stared down at the table.

"Nausea, weight gain, insomnia." She ticked off the points. "They're all common side effects. Sometimes they're worse than the disease."

Ben appreciated her intent, but he wasn't buying her rationale. "My father said her antidepressant worked great."

"Then maybe she thought she didn't need them anymore. It could be something as simple as that."

"Yeah, maybe," Ben said.

"Or maybe your father is wrong," Sierra said.

His head jerked up. "Excuse me?"

"He doesn't know for sure what happened at the overlook. Nobody does. She could have slipped and fallen, the same way the newspaper reported."

"I wish there was a way to know for sure." He'd investigated dozens of stories since getting the job at the *Tribune* and couldn't remember the truth eluding him on a single one. "The not knowing, that's the hardest part."

She reached across the table and covered his hand instead of pointing out he'd have to live with the uncertainty. She was special, he thought.

"I wish—" he began.

"Here you go." Ellie Marson arrived with his plate of scrambled eggs and bacon, setting the food in front of him. "Can I get anything else for you, hon?"

"No, thanks," he said.

Ellie left them to check on a slender redhead dining alone a few tables from them. Ben had noticed her earlier because she was watching them over the pages of her book.

"What do you wish?" Sierra asked, reclaiming his attention.

He wished they could explore what was developing between them, that Indigo Springs wasn't such a long drive from Pittsburgh, that their time together wasn't reaching an end.

"I wish we'd met under different circumstances." He turned his hand over, pressing their palms together, feeling the warmth of her skin, seeing it reflected in her eyes.

"Me, too." She sounded as though she really meant it. "I also wish I could stay while you finish breakfast, but I'm already late. If I don't get to the office soon, Missy will not be happy."

"Missy?"

"Missy Cromartie, our receptionist. She's gets the backlash when we run behind schedule."

"You should go, then." He tried a smile, didn't quite manage to pull one off. "You don't need to be treating your receptionist for high blood pressure."

She scooted partway across the booth, then stopped. "I'll probably have to work through lunch." She hesitated. "Will you still be in town when I'm done for the day?"

Everything inside him rebelled at the thought of leaving Indigo Springs today. Despite all that had happened, he wasn't ready to tell Sierra goodbye.

"I'll be here," he said. "You can call me on my cell when you're through. Give me your phone and I'll enter the number."

She waited while he punched his information into her cell. Their fingers brushed when he handed the phone back to her.

"Thanks." He locked eyes with her. "For everything."

He stared down at his plate of food when she was gone, his appetite nonexistent. Despite the crash course Sierra had given him on antidepressants, he had to face the very real possibility his mother jumped from that cliff.

The redhead who'd been watching them got up from her table and smoothed the skirt of her long, summer dress. She glanced over, then looked quickly away.

Wonder what that's about, he thought and decided to find out. Following his instincts had paid off more than once.

"Excuse me." He caught up to her between two vacant tables. "I couldn't help noticing you looking at me. Do we know each other?"

She gazed down at her feet, then snuck another glance at him. "I saw you at the library," she said in a whisper more commonly heard inside a library than a restaurant.

It was unlike him not to notice the people around him, yet she was unfamiliar. "When was that?"

"I was shelving books near the reference desk when you asked Mrs. Wiesneski about that computer log."

The log that didn't exist. He'd timed his return to the

library to coincide with Mrs. Wiesneski's day off, hoping to find a more forthcoming source. Her coworker had verified no records were kept of the people who used the public-access computers.

"I'm not sure how I missed you," Ben said. "I tried to talk to everyone who works there."

"Oh, I don't work at the library," she said in the same quiet voice. "I'm just there all the time since my computer started acting up. Sometimes I help out, kind of like a thank-you."

"Were you at the library last Friday?" he asked.

"I'm there every day," she said.

His optimism waned. If she visited the library all the time, the days probably blurred one into another.

"I don't suppose you remember who else was using the public-access computers last Friday?" Ben asked, fully expecting to slam into another wall.

"On the contrary," she said in a confident, steady voice, "I remember perfectly."

CHAPTER ELEVEN

SIERRA GLANCED DOWN at the patient's name on the file folder she plucked from the holder affixed to the exam room door. After leaving Ben, she'd feared it would be difficult to focus on work.

She suspected that Laurie Grieb, however, would present a stimulating challenge.

"Hi, Laurie." She shut the door behind her after entering the room and focused on the young woman who sat on the exam table, her long legs dangling in space. "What brings you into the office today?"

"As if you didn't know," Laurie grumbled.

"Excuse me?" Sierra wasn't well enough acquainted with Laurie to pick up on her moods.

"Sara said you told her to make an appointment and let me know when it was," Laurie said.

Sierra set Laurie's chart down on the flat surface of the desk while she considered how to deal with her reluctant patient. Honesty seemed the best approach. "Sara says you haven't been feeling well. She's worried about you."

"I love her, but she should mind her own business," Laurie snapped. Despite the strength in her words, her face appeared overly pale beneath her long, curly hair.

Smudges shadowed the area under her brown eyes. "I can take care of myself."

Sierra had witnessed Ben valiantly hiding his pain so recently it wasn't difficult to recognize Laurie doing the same thing. Ben's pain hadn't been physical. Her guess was that Laurie's wasn't, either.

"If you can take care of yourself," Sierra asked evenly, "what are you doing here?"

"Excuse me?"

"In my experience, people who aren't worried about their health don't come to the doctor. No matter who makes the appointment."

Laurie's brave face crumbled. Her lips trembled and she blinked a few times to keep the tears shimmering in her eyes from falling.

"What's going on, Laurie?" Sierra prompted.

"I'll be thirty next year. When my aunt was thirty, she was diagnosed with leukemia. She died two years later." Now that Laurie had started to talk, her words came fast and furious. "I'm nauseous and tired all the time. I looked it up on the Web, and those are some of the early symptoms of leukemia."

"Let's not get ahead of ourselves." Sierra made herself speak calmly. "Those could be the symptoms of a lot of other things, too. Has your period been late?"

"Well, yeah, but I'm irregular."

"Is it possible you're pregnant?"

Laurie's long hair swung when she shook her head. "Me and Kenny—that's my ex-husband who'll be my husband again once we get around to remarrying—use birth control."

"Birth control isn't one hundred percent effective."

"You don't understand. We've been really careful. I was pregnant the first time we got married and everything fell apart when I miscarried. This time we're waiting to have kids until we're sure we're ready."

Sierra mentally filed away that information and approached the exam table, unwilling to jump to conclusions before she had all the facts. "I'm going to listen to your heart and check out a couple of other things."

When she was through with the examination, she stood back and said, "Everything checks out so far. I'm going to need a urine sample from you. Then I'll have a nurse come in and draw blood."

Fear shone out of Laurie's eyes.

Sierra touched her on the arm. "Try not to worry, Laurie. Drawing blood is standard procedure when a patient complains of fatigue. We'll send the sample to the lab for processing and get the results in a few days."

"That long?" Laurie moaned. "I'm not sure I can be that patient."

It turned out she didn't need to be, because the urine test solved the medical mystery. She was pregnant.

Laurie's eyes bugged and her mouth popped open at the news. "I can't be pregnant. Kenny and I use protection."

"Whatever you're using, it's not one hundred percent effective because you're definitely expecting," Sierra said. "I rechecked the results myself."

"But...but..." Laurie placed trembling hands over her mouth and burst into tears.

Sierra hurried to her side, putting a hand on the other

woman's arm to comfort her. Laurie threw herself at Sierra, sobbing in earnest.

"It's okay, Laurie." Sierra patted her on the back. "You haven't even told Kenny yet. Once you talk it over with him, the news might not seem so overwhelming."

Laurie drew back, fat tears streaming down her face. "You think I don't want to be pregnant?"

"You are crying," Sierra pointed out.

"I'm crying because I'm so happy I can't stand it." Laurie gave her a watery smile. "The saddest day of my life was when I lost Kenny's baby."

Sierra's head felt like it was spinning. "Didn't you just say you were determined not to get pregnant?"

"When you know me better, you'll realize you shouldn't listen to everything I say. I talk *a lot.* Believe this, though. It feels like a miracle that I'm pregnant. With Kenny's baby." She threw her head back and laughed through the tears. "I'm pregnant with Kenny's baby!"

Sierra laughed with her, easily able to envision how wonderful it would be to carry the child of the man you loved.

Because she loved Ben Nash.

Her laughter stopped as abruptly as it had started, shocked into submission by the ludicrous thought. She hadn't even known Ben a week. How could she possibly entertain the notion that she loved him?

Because she did, a voice inside her head answered. She immediately shut it out.

Love didn't just sneak up on a person and blindside them. It needed to be nurtured and grown, further proof that what she felt wasn't love.

Passion, she thought. It must be passion.

The label she put on the feeling didn't matter. She'd never tell him. Speaking of loving Ben Nash aloud would be crazy.

"I can't wait to tell him!" Laurie announced.

Sierra nearly shouted at her to keep quiet, then felt silly. Laurie wasn't referring to Ben Nash. She was talking about informing her husband about the treasured baby. The other woman couldn't possibly know about the crazy thoughts that had just run though Sierra's head.

"You go do that," Sierra said.

Laurie took her literally, practically sprinting out of the exam room. Sierra followed, calling, "Wait. I wasn't finished. You need to call your ob-gyn ASAP to schedule an appointment."

Ryan glanced up from where he sat at the desk in the hall, pausing in the act of writing a prescription.

"I'm pregnant!" Laurie announced.

Ryan gave her a thumbs-up. "Way to go!"

Laurie giggled, then told Sierra, "My ob-gyn is in Harrisburg. I never got around to getting one in town after I moved back here."

"Ask Missy to give you the address and phone number for Dr. Nekoba on your way out of the office," Sierra said. "I can recommend him highly."

"I know his contact information by heart." Ryan tore a sheet from his prescription pad and jotted down the doctor's name and phone number. "Here you go."

Laurie took the sheet, thanked him and hurried away, a skip in her step.

"Missy's not at the reception desk," Ryan said quietly when Laurie was out of earshot. "I saw her heading up the stairs about five minutes ago."

The office building boasted a rooftop terrace that had been a major selling point when their father relocated his headquarters. He used to say he spent so much time working, it was imperative he have a place to recharge and clear his head during office hours.

Their employees often took breaks on the terrace when the weather allowed. Today, however, was blustery with the threat of rain.

"It's too early for her break," Sierra said, thinking aloud. "Why would she go up there now?"

"I thought you might know," Ryan said, then added the kicker. "Because Ben Nash went with her."

WIND GUSTED OVER the irregularly shaped rooftops of the buildings in downtown Indigo Springs, carrying the heavy scent of rain. In the distance, the lush green peaks and valleys of the Poconos rippled against the darkening sky.

On another morning, the terrace would be the perfect spot to take in the beauty of the surroundings. Today, the patio furniture would blow away if it weren't made of stone. The potted plants bent over sideways.

"We should go back inside," Ben said.

"No!" The word erupted from Missy, even as she held her shoulder-length hair back from her face with one hand. "If Dr. Sierra or Dr. Ryan find out what we're talking about, I might lose my job. And I really, really need this job."

"Then you know why I'm here?" Ben hadn't had a chance to tell her yet. When she'd found out he was at the office to talk to her, she'd quickly led him to the terrace.

"It's about the e-mails, isn't it?" she asked in a loud whisper. "You know I sent them."

Until that moment, Ben had some doubts that the young lady he'd met at Jimmy's Diner was right about who she'd seen using the library computer. He'd assumed mountaindweller was a contemporary of Dr. Whitmore's. Missy Cromartie was barely out of high school.

"Yes," Ben said. "I just don't know why."

"Isn't it obvious?" She had a overly dramatic way about her, with an expressive face and a voice that dipped and peaked. "I wanted you to investigate whether Dr. Whitmore had anything to do with your mom's death."

"How do you know Allison Blaine was my mother?"

"It's super easy to find out stuff like that on the Internet. You'd know all about that. I mean, you work for a newspaper, right?"

He wasn't doing the greatest job of getting to the bottom of things at the moment. He still hadn't figured out her motivation.

"I didn't even know old Dr. Whitmore," Missy said. "I was only hired about a year ago after I dropped out of community college. School just wasn't for me. I was lucky to get a job at all. I probably wouldn't have if my grandma hadn't been a nurse here for so many years."

Her grandmother. Now they were getting somewhere. The grandmother must be the connection.

"Did your grandmother tell you to e-mail me?" Ben asked.

"Grandma died last month." Missy blinked a few times, sniffled and continued talking. "But I guess you could say that."

She let go of her hair to rub at her nose. Wind gusted over the rooftop, bringing with it some plump raindrops and rattling the leaves in the planters. The strands of Missy's dark hair completely obscured her face.

"Let's go inside." This time Ben didn't give her a choice, crossing to the door and holding it open for her. The wind practically blew them inside onto a small landing at the top of a staircase that descended into the office. He pulled the door shut behind them to find Missy staying put. She was so tiny, she had to crane her neck to look up at him.

"Before Grandma died, she asked if I'd get in contact with your family," she told him in a hushed voice that was still fairly loud. "It really must have bothered her that she didn't tell someone what she suspected." She paused, as if for dramatic effect.

"What exactly did she suspect?"

"That's just it," Missy said. "Grandma wasn't sure. She just knew something wasn't right."

Ben tried not to let on how frustrated he was with her roundabout way of telling a story. "How did she know that?"

"Because of what Dr. Whitmore did with your mom's blood sample," she said in the same loud whisper.

Ben stopped breathing. Alex Rawlings had mentioned having tests run after his mother died, but hadn't revealed who'd extracted the sample. He should have guessed it had been Dr. Whitmore. It was routine for the physicians in small towns to take on the duties of medical examiners.

"What happened with her blood sample?" he prompted.

"Dr. Whitmore told the police chief the sample was normal, but that might not have been true." Missy's eyes got so big they seemed to take up a third of her face. "Grandma knew she should have said something, but Dr. Whitmore was so good to her. And such a good man, too."

Ben waited for the punch line, but she'd paused again. He'd have to ask. "Why didn't she believe the sample was normal?"

"Because she saw Dr. Whitmore switching the label on the blood sample he sent to the lab. Whoever's blood came back clean, it wasn't your mother's."

A gasp sounded, but it didn't come from Ben. He descended the stairs and found Sierra between the second and third floors with her back plastered against a wall. Her pallor was as white as her lab coat.

Ben rushed to her side and placed a hand on her arm. "Are you okay?"

She said nothing.

Footsteps thundered behind them. It was Missy, traipsing down the stairs. "Oh, no! Dr. Sierra, I didn't know you were there! Please believe me, I didn't mean to cause trouble. I can explain everything. Just please don't fire me."

"You can explain later," Ben told the receptionist. He took an unresisting Sierra by the hand, navigated the last bank of stairs and emerged in the office. He headed for the long hallway lined with the examination rooms. A nurse walked toward them, her white shoes making squishing sounds on the carpet, her lips parted as she started to say something.

"Give us a minute, okay?" Ben spoke before the nurse could. He ushered Sierra inside a vacant exam room and shut the door on the woman's surprised face.

"You look like you need time to compose yourself." He led Sierra to a stationary chair in the corner of the room. She sank into it. He wheeled another chair in front of her and sat down, his legs spread, his forearms balanced on his thighs. "What Missy said must have come as a shock."

The receptionist's revelation had surprised him, too, even though on some level he'd known from the start that Sierra's father—her *beloved* father—wasn't innocent. Although he couldn't fathom why Dr. Whitmore hadn't wanted his patient's blood analyzed, the reason had to be the key to everything.

"I don't believe it." When Sierra finally spoke, it seemed as though she was talking to herself.

"I know it was hard to hear," he said gently, "but Missy has no reason to lie."

"I didn't mean I don't believe Missy." Her voice gained steam. "I don't believe her grandmother."

He ran a hand through his short hair, trying to put himself in her shocked place while he thought about how to respond. "It was a deathbed confession, Sierra.

Missy's grandmother couldn't take that information with her to the grave. How can you believe she was lying?"

"I didn't say she was lying." She focused on him, her eyes intense. "She probably even thought she saw my father switching that sample, but she didn't."

"How could you know that?" he asked incredulously.

"My father wouldn't do something like that."

"Wow." Ben kept his gaze steady on her, feeling as though he was seeing her clearly for the first time. "I knew you liked to create your own fiction, but I didn't know how bad it was."

"What's that supposed to mean?"

"Come on, Sierra. Ever since I got to town, you haven't been interested in the truth. The only thing important to you is preserving your father's reputation."

"No." The color in her face deepened. She stood up and glared at him. "It's not allowing you to damage his reputation. There's a difference."

Ben got out of his chair, too. They faced off, like combatants.

"I couldn't do any damage if there was nothing to find out," he said. "You need to accept that your father had flaws. Serious flaws."

"You don't know the first thing about my father!"

"I know he's the reason you aren't leading the kind of life that would make you happy."

"That's ridiculous!"

"Is it? Not long ago, you told me how lucky I was to live in a big city. You never would have come back here after your residency if not for your father."

"I came back to go into practice with him."

"That's what *you* wanted to happen," Ben said, then repeated what Ryan had told him when they'd had lunch together in the park. "Your father wanted your brother to take over his practice."

She looked as if he'd thrown a baseball at her and hit her in the stomach. "That's a low blow."

He couldn't let her pain sway him. She needed to hear what he had to say. "It's the truth and deep down you know it, just like you know this life you've built isn't what you want."

Her eyes glittered. "So now you're an expert on me even though we haven't known each other a week."

"I've seen more of your real self in that week than you showed Armstrong in all the years you dated."

She threw up a hand. "I can't believe you're bringing Chad into it."

"Why not?" he said. "You built up a fiction around him, too. You convinced yourself you loved him."

"I did love him."

"You loved the idea of a man your father approved of. If you were honest with yourself, you would have been the one to break things off." He looked around the room for something to illustrate his point and made a sweeping gesture with his right hand. "Armstrong is as wrong for you as that doorknob."

"I guess now you're going to say *you're* right for me?" She took a few steps forward and glared up at him.

"I wasn't. But now that you bring it up, yeah, it makes a hell of a lot more sense for you to be with me."

"The man trying to ruin my father's good name," she bit out.

"The man determined to get at the truth," he retorted.

"So you're going to pursue this, even after what your father told you?"

"Damn right I am," he said. "Your father switching the blood sample proves there's more to the story. I'm going to find out what it is."

"You haven't been able to establish my father even met your mother."

"I've been thinking about that." The seeds of his theory had been planted when Connor told the story about hitting his head. Alex Rawlings had mentioned that his brother was a hellion. What if the incident happened in Indigo Springs? "I know your father didn't treat patients under eighteen. But what if the pediatrician was closed? Wouldn't your father have been available in an emergency?"

She peered at him with blatant suspicion. "What are you getting at?"

"We only looked under the name Blaine when we checked your files," he said. "If my mother brought one of my brothers here, the record would be under Nash."

"I'm not going back into the records," she said. "I won't help you grab at straws. Besides, it wouldn't prove a thing even if she had been in the office."

"It would prove they'd met."

"So what? It's a dead end, Ben."

He shoved aside his frustration, dropping that angle to come at the investigation another way. "I still need to find out why your mother claimed your father was out of town."

"I already told you why. She remembered wrong."

"Then maybe I can jog her memory. When do you expect her back from Atlantic City?"

Sierra grew silent. He could almost see the gears in her brain turning. Finally, she said, "They're both gone, Ben. Does it really matter what happened nineteen years ago?"

"Of course it does," he said. "The truth always matters."

"And you'll stop at nothing to get to it?"

Nobody had ever posed that question to Ben before. He'd built his entire adult life on ferreting out secrets. He'd gone into journalism to accomplish that goal.

"That's right," he said.

"At what cost?"

"Excuse me?"

"What if I asked you to leave my mother alone?" Sierra asked, her voice catching. "If you really are the man for me, you'd do that for me."

Her request sliced into him, coming perilously close to his heart.

"If you were the woman for me," he finally responded, "you wouldn't ask me to."

He took one last long look at her, then turned and went, because there was nothing left to say.

CHAPTER TWELVE

SIERRA REMAINED BEHIND the closed doors of the examination room, her adrenaline running so rampant she was literally shaking.

How dare Ben say those things to her! He hadn't known her father. If he had, he'd realize how off base his accusations were. As for his assertion that he was the right man for her, she wouldn't even think about it.

What was important right now was protecting her father's reputation. She simply couldn't give credence to the accusation that he'd falsified evidence. The reason she hadn't agreed to check the old files was simple. Why help Ben drum up suspicion where there should be none?

Three quick knocks sounded on the door before it swung open, admitting her brother. He cocked his head, regarding her closely.

"Everything okay?" Ryan asked. "Ben just stormed out of here, and Missy looks like she's about to hyperventilate."

Sierra got her shakes under control before she spoke. "Missy thinks we're going to fire her," she said, then told her brother everything.

He listened without interrupting, then said, "It doesn't make sense that Dad would falsify evidence."

"Exactly!" Sierra retorted. "He didn't even know the woman."

"If you're so sure of that, I don't understand why you wouldn't check to see if Dad treated one of Ben's brothers."

"Because I didn't want to give him ammunition!"

"If you're putting it in those terms, you could have taken the gun away from him. He couldn't fire at Dad if the file isn't there."

"Dr. Ryan! Where are you?" Their nurse practitioner's voice traveled down the hall.

"Duty calls," Ryan said. "Since Janine's here today, we can both cover for you if you need time to deal with all of this."

Sierra eyes misted at his offer. To think that not even a year ago, they'd only spoken to each other at infrequent family gatherings.

"I don't know if I've ever told you this before," Sierra said, her voice thick with emotion, "but you're a really good brother."

"You never have," he said, "but now's a really good time to start."

He winked at her and went to tend to their patients, leaving her to think about what he'd said. If Ben was determined to build a case against her father, she should be armed with a defense. Her father's files could cast serious doubt on whether he'd been acquainted with Allison Blaine.

Walking quickly out the door and through the hall

so nobody would intercept her, she let herself into the room where they kept the noncomputerized records.

She yanked open the correct file drawer and located the *N*s. The trembles came back as she thumbed through the tabs, searching for the last name Nash.

Nothing, just as she'd suspected. She closed her eyes, feeling relief flood over her.

She was about to shut the file drawer when she spotted a folder slightly lower than the rest that she'd bypassed the first time around. She tugged it free. *Nash, Connor,* it read.

She sucked in a breath, trying to recall if Ben had ever told her the names of his brothers. She didn't think so. She exhaled. Just because a file existed for a Connor Nash didn't mean he was related to Ben. The last name Nash was common enough.

She pulled out the file and slowly opened it. The patient, Connor Nash, had been four years old at the time of the treatment. He'd been brought into the office because of a bump on his head.

Agreed to see patient because Dr. Goldstein unavailable, her father had scribbled in the notes field of the chart, referring to the pediatrician who'd practiced in town for as long as Sierra could remember. *Patient exhibits no signs of concussion. Instructions are to keep a watch on him and follow up with Dr. Goldstein. No treatment necessary.*

She flipped to the information sheet that must be filled out before any patient could be seen. The signature at the bottom was flowing and easy to read: Allison Blaine.

The room swayed and her legs felt as though they might buckle. She anchored her hand on the top of the file cabinet and breathed in and out. She turned around, half fearing someone would be looking over her shoulder at the incriminating evidence. No one was there.

She immediately expelled the word *incriminating* from her head. Like she'd told Ben, it would mean nothing if her father and his mother had a chance encounter.

Then why had Sierra's mother insisted her husband had never met Allison Blaine? The woman's death had been well-publicized. Wouldn't her parents have discussed it among themselves? Wouldn't her father have mentioned Allison Blaine had been in the office with her young son?

The questions crowded Sierra's brain, making it difficult to think. Only one woman had the answers.

She dug her cell phone from the pocket of her lab coat and held down the number that speed-dialed her mother's phone. The phone rang. And rang.

"Pick up, Mom," Sierra said aloud.

By Sierra's calculations, Rosemary Whitmore's tour bus should have left Atlantic City by now. That didn't mean she'd answer the phone. Half the time she didn't even have the thing turned on.

Just when she was about to give up, she heard her mother's voice. "Hello."

"Mom. Where are you?"

"What? I can't hear you."

Sierra could barely make out her mother's voice amid the background noise. The buzz of conversation mingled with the hum of what sounded like a motor. "Are you on the bus?"

"No," her mother answered loudly. "I'm on the bus."

So much for trying to have a conversation. Sierra attempted another question. "When will you be home?"

"I'm hanging up, Sierra." Her mother obviously hadn't heard a word. "Call me when I get home. Probably around noon."

Her mother disconnected the call, leaving Sierra listening to silence. She clicked off her phone, then considered what to do. Her mother planned to drive to Indigo Springs later today after she returned from the Atlantic City trip.

If Sierra waited to talk to her, however, she risked the possibility Ben would get to her mother first.

She couldn't afford to let that happen.

SIERRA PACED THE sidewalk in front of the main clubhouse at the Mountain Village Estates forty-five minutes later, uncaring that a cool drizzle was falling from the cloudy sky.

The roar of a motor finally sounded in the distance, followed by the appearance of one of the sleek gray buses the retirement community chartered for its frequent excursions.

The residents who had taken the Atlantic City trip filed off the bus, most of them laughing. They'd either had good luck in the casinos or enough money their losses didn't sting.

Rosemary Whitmore was among the last to disembark. Her mother's somewhat formal clothing—cocoa-brown slacks and a cream-colored jacket—contrasted with the blue jeans worn by the unfamiliar white-haired woman with whom she was speaking.

Her mother looked up and spotted Sierra. She stopped talking, seemingly in midsentence, then said something to the other woman before moving toward her daughter on high-heeled shoes. "Sierra, what are you doing here? Is something wrong? Is it Ryan? Is he okay?"

"Ryan's fine, Mom," Sierra said quickly. "I just need to talk to you."

"Didn't you remember I'm coming to Indigo Springs today?"

"I need to talk to you about Dad," Sierra clarified. She took a breath before continuing. "And about Allison Blaine."

A wariness Sierra didn't want to acknowledge settled over her mother. "I told your young man. Your father never met her." Her tone was almost haughty.

"Did Dad tell you that?" Sierra asked.

Her mother went still and seemed to weigh her next words. "Why do you ask?"

"Dad treated one of Ben's brothers when Dr. Goldstein wasn't available," Sierra said. "Allison Blaine brought him into the office. The form she filled out is in her son's chart."

Even without sunlight illuminating her mother's face, Sierra picked up on the way her complexion whitened. The older woman closed her eyes and shook her head. "I forgot about that boy's chart."

Sierra's heartbeat sped up. "Then you knew Dad was in town when Ben's mother died?"

"His mother?" She blew a breath out of her nose. "That explains why he's so interested in something that happened so many years ago. I should have figured that out myself."

"You didn't answer the question," Sierra said.

"Yes," her mother said. "I knew."

Sierra's lungs deflated, momentarily robbing her of oxygen. "Then why did you lie?"

"I had to." Her mother lowered her voice even though nobody was within hearing distance. "I couldn't let that reporter turn her death into something it wasn't."

Too much of this didn't make sense. Sierra briefly told her mother about the allegation Missy Cromartie said her grandmother had made.

Her mother's face tightened. She glanced around at their surroundings. The drizzle had gotten heavier. The small groups of residents who had been saying their goodbyes were now hurrying to escape the rain, some heading to nearby condos, others to the cars they'd left in the parking lot.

"Do you still want that ride, Rosemary?" called the white-haired lady in jeans.

"No thanks, Helen. My daughter will take me home." She waved to her friend, then put a hand on Sierra's back, moving her toward the car. "Don't say anything else here."

Sierra used the few moments it took to drive to her mother's condo to get her thoughts in order. Her mother seemed content to travel in silence. Even inside the condo, her mother was in no hurry to start the conversation.

"Wait for me in the sunroom," her mother suggested, then opened blinds and turned on lights to counteract the gloomy day. It was raining in earnest now. The golf course was deserted except for a lone Canadian goose that waddled on the fairway.

Sierra was attempting to convince herself a logical explanation would be forthcoming when her mother joined her, occupying the same seat Ben had when he'd visited.

"Tell me everything that happened this morning," her mother said. "Don't leave out anything."

Sierra put her questions on hold. Once she had her answers, she had a sickening feeling her life would never be the same. She relayed the events of the morning, ending with Ben's second request to check their old records.

Her mother laid a finger against her chin. "Then you can conveniently *misplace* the Nash boy's file."

"Why would I do that?"

"To protect your father's name, of course. I thought you understood that."

"To protect him from what?" Sierra asked sharply, no longer able to stand the way her mother was dancing around the subject. In a smaller voice, she added, "If you don't explain soon, I'll think he did switch the label on that blood sample."

Her mother's mouth shook and her face crumbled. "Under the circumstances, it was the only thing he could do."

A patient of Sierra's had once described what the electric shock felt like when she'd been struck by lightning. Sierra experienced something like that now. She couldn't form words, not even to ask the obvious question.

"If he hadn't done it," her mother continued after long moments, "somebody would have questioned the drugs in her system. They might have traced it back to your father."

Sierra struggled to find her voice. "That doesn't make sense. Allison Blaine wasn't Dad's patient. A doctor in Pittsburgh put her on antidepressants."

"I haven't told you everything yet," her mother said. "After your father told her that her son was okay, she asked him to give her something for her migraines."

Sierra's heart started to pound in earnest.

"The office was behind schedule because he'd squeezed in the boy. The people in the waiting room were getting impatient. He gave her some samples he had in the office without checking her medical history. They were only supposed to tide her over until she could make an appointment."

Her mother's story started to make terrible sense. Allison Blaine had been taking an SSRI, a popular class of antidepressant medications.

"Were the samples triptans?" Sierra named a family of drugs commonly prescribed for migraines.

"Yes," her mother said.

Her heart squeezed. When taken together, the two drugs could carry a grave risk.

"Dad was afraid her blood would show a high level of serotonin," Sierra said, thinking aloud. Serotonin was a neurotransmitter that helped relay signals from one area of the brain to another.

"That's right," her mother said. "Your father said the combination could have caused some sort of syndrome."

Serotonin syndrome could lead to restlessness, confusion and even loss of muscle coordination. If Allison Blaine had been afflicted, it would explain why her car had been weaving across the center line of the road near the overlook. The horror of her father's mistake penetrated Sierra's numbed mind.

"Dad thought the drug interactions could explain a fall from a cliff," Sierra said.

Rosemary nodded unhappily. "I told him he couldn't know that for sure. She was alone so maybe she did jump. But he blamed himself for giving her those samples without asking what other drugs she was taking."

"He should have gone to Alex Rawlings and confessed what he'd done," Sierra said.

"He wanted to, but I begged him not to," her mother said. "Allison Blaine was already gone. Nothing he did would bring her back. I finally persuaded him to switch the label."

"*You* got him to switch?"

"I had to. You heard me. I couldn't let him throw away his career and ruin his reputation on something that might not even have been his fault. It could have destroyed our family."

"It wasn't your place to make that determination," Sierra said. "He falsified evidence."

"It was the right thing to do," her mother insisted stubbornly. "Look what good he did as a doctor, what good he did in the community. He couldn't have done any of that if he'd lost his license."

Sierra doubted it would have come to that. Even if

her father had been facing career ruin, it didn't excuse what he'd done. "It was still wrong."

"Don't you think he knew that? That's why he had a problem with alcohol."

Sierra couldn't ever remember seeing her father drunk. "Dad didn't drink too much," she denied.

"He was careful never to overindulge in public or in front of you and Ryan, but he most certainly did," her mother said. "Why do you think he went to the basement to sneak drinks?"

Her father had kept a flask hidden in his basement office, something Sierra had discovered while she was in high school. "Because you didn't like him drinking."

"That's right," her mother said. "I knew it wasn't good for him. Turns out I was right. He was under doctor's orders not to drink after his first heart attack but that didn't stop him."

That was news to Sierra, who had been in college when her father suffered his initial heart attack.

"Don't you see, Sierra?" her mother continued. "That mistake haunted your father. He paid for his mistake when he was alive. It wouldn't serve any purpose to reveal it now."

Sierra detected the flaw in her mother's reasoning, even with her mind reeling from what she'd learned. "What about Ben's father? He thinks his wife committed suicide."

"Maybe she did," her mother said.

"More likely she didn't," Sierra argued. "Don't you think Ben and his family have a right to know something else might have happened?"

As a doctor, she'd dealt with the aftermath of death enough times to know how a survivor's mind worked. If Ben eventually accepted his father's theory, he might never get past the feeling his mother hadn't loved her family enough to fight to stay alive.

"*Might* have, Sierra," her mother said. "Why stir things up?"

"Ben's stirring things up all by himself," she pointed out. "He knows Dad played in the Lakeview Pines golf tournament the week his mother died."

"That's not proof, and neither is anything your receptionist told him," her mother said. "He has no way to verify anything."

Sierra's head hurt. She realized she was clenching her jaw. "You talk like he's the enemy."

"Listen to me, Sierra Whitmore." Her mother's voice was steely. "Your father spent his life making up for that single mistake. He has a right to be remembered for the good he did with his life. That's what your focus should be on. Not on some man you barely know."

A man who'd gotten her to open up to him in ways she'd never dreamed possible. He claimed he knew the real Sierra.

Could that woman live with herself if she failed to enlighten him about the past that continued to haunt him?

A FEW EXCRUCIATING hours later, Sierra let herself out of her childhood home, where Ryan now lived with Annie, her mother's voice ringing in her ears.

"You can't tell him, Sierra," Rosemary Whitmore had said over and over again. "Think about your father."

If Sierra had anticipated her mother would continually return to the subject of Ben Nash, she wouldn't have agreed to drive her to Indigo Springs.

She breathed deeply of air washed clean by the rain, glad to be free of her mother's stifling presence. Relieved, too, that Ryan had insisted she needn't bother returning to work.

She craved time alone to think. To process the ramifications of the disastrous mistake her father had made.

Her father, who hadn't been perfect after all.

She looked toward the street, her feet freezing at the sight of the silver convertible at the curb. Ben emerged, his determination evident in his tall, proud carriage.

His gait didn't falter when he spotted her. He kept coming, closing the ground between them until he stood at the bottom of the stairs. His lean face appeared haggard, his eyes hooded.

The time of reckoning was upon her.

"I came to see if your mother was in town yet." His monotone belied everything that had passed between them. "Ryan said he expected her today."

"She's inside," Sierra said.

His squint wasn't caused by the sun, which was still obscured by the clouds. "I see."

"What do you see?"

He shrugged stiffly. "You tracked your mother down and warned her about the questions I'd ask. Tell me something, Sierra, is it worth it for me to talk to her now?"

His implication couldn't have been more clear. "You think I told her what to say."

"Didn't you?" He didn't seem angry or disappointed. He sounded…hurt.

His pain reached out to her until she felt it, too. She needed no more time to think about what to do with her information. All along, there had been only one viable choice.

"You're right. It's no use talking to my mother. She won't tell you anything." She was so attuned to his reactions she felt him wince. "But I will."

From the flatlining of his lips and hardening of his features, it was easy to see he didn't trust her. She had only herself to blame.

She sank onto the porch at the top of the steps, feeling the dampness from the recent rain penetrate the back of her skirt. Yet another expensive garment she cared little if she ruined.

He stood without moving for a few moments, looking like an implacable force, then climbed the three steps. He lowered himself so that he sat beside her and yet held himself apart, silently communicating what her reluctance to face facts had done to them. The residential neighborhood was virtually deserted at this time of the afternoon. The only sounds were the chirping of birds, the distant bark of a dog and her shallow breaths.

"I know the truth," she said.

She proceeded to tell him, omitting nothing. She spared neither her mother nor her father, refusing to make excuses for them. He didn't look at her as she talked, giving her the impression he couldn't see anything but the past.

"So my father was wrong," he said in a thick voice when she finished. "My mother didn't kill herself."

"There's a convincing case to be made that she fell, just like you'd always been told." Sierra couldn't hold back. She needed him to have all the details, no matter how poorly they reflected on her father. "In some cases, the interaction of SSRI antidepressants and triptans can lead to confusion and disorientation."

"In some cases?" he asked.

"There's no way to know for sure what effect the drugs had on her," Sierra said. "That's how my mother convinced my father to switch the label on the blood sample. I doubt he fully bought into her argument, though."

"Why do you say that?"

"Your mother was seen driving erratically, which suggests she was suffering from side effects. It's easy to imagine her getting too close to the edge of the cliff and falling. But logic isn't the only reason I think my father blamed himself."

"What's the other one?"

"I wrote his biography for the festival," she said. "He didn't get involved in community service until after your mother died. My mother says he was trying to atone for his sin."

She swallowed the lump of emotion that had crept into her throat. "You were right. I built up this fiction around my father, just like you said. I found out today he had a drinking problem. I didn't even know that."

His response was slow in coming. "Everybody has flaws."

"Not as serious as the ones my father had." She drew a deep breath. "I understand you're a reporter and you have to write the story about what my father did. I don't have any right to ask this of you, but I'm going to anyway."

He said nothing, just waited for her to finish.

"I couldn't bear for my family to have to deal with the publicity during the festival." She knew the enormity of what she was asking. Considering the obstacles she'd put in Ben's way as he chased after the truth, he owed her no favors. "Will you wait until after the festival to publish the story?"

Before he could refuse, she rushed to add reassurances. "I realize it would be hypocritical to allow my father to be honored." Her voice cracked. "I promise to make sure the park won't be named for him."

She could feel the *thud-thud-thud* of her heart as she waited for his answer. Her stomach rolled with nausea. It seemed a very long time before he said, "Why did you tell me this? If you hadn't, I wouldn't have found out."

They were sitting perhaps a foot apart, not touching, yet she could feel the heat of his body. She finally looked him full in the face, only to find his eyes trained on her.

"It was something you said about wishing your mother had fought harder to stay alive." She blew out a breath. "I didn't want you to go through the rest of your life believing she didn't love you enough."

There was another reason she'd come clean that was just as compelling: She loved him.

Every other time the notion crept into her head, she'd discounted it on the basis she couldn't love a man after so short an acquaintance.

She didn't reject it now.

It was ironic that she'd waited to own up to her feelings until he had good reason to shun her. She swallowed in an effort to open her clogged windpipe and strove to keep the tremble from her voice.

"Will you honor my request?" Her voice cracked, despite her best efforts. "Will you hold the story until after the festival?"

His nod, when it came, was slow. "I can do that."

She rose on stiff legs from the porch. Quite suddenly, there was nothing more to say except, "Thank you."

He nodded in acknowledgement.

She brushed off the bottom of her damp skirt and made the long, lonely trek to where she'd parked in the driveway. Before she got into her car, she surrendered to the overwhelming temptation to glance back at him. His head was bowed, his shoulders slumped. She longed to comfort him, but didn't have the right.

He must have sensed her watching because he lifted his head before raising one hand in farewell.

She waved back, then turned away.

It was, quite possibly, the last time she'd ever see him.

CHAPTER THIRTEEN

THE NEWSROOM OF the *Pittsburgh Tribune* was unnaturally quiet when Ben stepped off the elevator on Friday morning, the carpet muting even his footsteps. Only a few cubicles were occupied, the clacking of computer keyboards nearly too soft to be heard.

Maybe the office was always slow to come to life. Ben wouldn't know. He'd never arrived much before ten o'clock. It was before eight now.

He wondered if Sierra was at work and how she was dealing with the disillusion of discovering her father's mistake.

He'd talked himself out of contacting her last night after he'd gotten back to his apartment and made the round of obligatory phone calls to his family. What could he have said to her? "You think you're feeling bad now? Wait until the article comes out where I assassinate your father's character."

"Nash." Larry Timmons, the young reporter who was working on the group-home story, came up behind him carrying a can of caffeinated soda. "I thought you were still on vacation."

So Joe Geraldi, the paper's managing editor, hadn't

revealed the real reason Ben had been missing in action. His relief didn't make much sense. Once the story was published, everybody would find out where he'd been and what he'd been doing.

"I'm back now," Ben said. "How's the story coming?"

The kid, who was dressed in jeans and looked like he hadn't had his hair cut in a year, twisted his mouth. "Not great. Joe keeps pushing and pushing but, I'm not convinced there's anything there."

"Really? How so?"

"The director of the place has this three-strikes policy causing all the problems," Larry said. "The people who've been kicked out allege they're getting a raw deal. At first it looked that way to me, too."

"How about now?"

"Now it's not so clear. There are only eight spaces in the house and a waiting list ten times that long. Yeah, the director's a little inflexible. He makes the argument he has to remove the people who don't fit in for the greater good. The mentally ill, they don't deal well with disruptions."

"What's your take on the guy?"

"He's not somebody I'd grab a beer with, but I like what he's about. He can't succeed with everyone so he's helping as many people as he can."

"Sounds to me like you're right," Ben said.

"You agree with me?" Larry shook his head. "Man, that's the last thing I expected from the Rottweiler."

None of his fellow reporters had ever used that nickname to Ben's face before.

"Yeah, well, I like to think I have a few surprises in me," Ben said. "Is Joe here?"

"If he wasn't, I wouldn't be. I'm supposed to meet with him in a few minutes."

"Mind if I talk to him first?"

"Go right ahead." Larry popped the tab on his soda and took a swig. "I need time to wake up."

The door to Joe's office was open. Ben knocked anyway, drawing the managing editor's attention from the morning newspaper. Surprise wreathed his face. "Well, damn, thanks for telling me you were coming."

"Hello to you, too," Ben said.

"You think I'm not glad to see you?" Joe shut the newspaper and got up from the desk, bringing with him an empty foam cup. "I'm so frigging overjoyed, your cup of coffee's on me."

Ben suspected Joe needed the caffeine more than he did. Everybody, even the reporters who didn't start work until well after dawn, knew the editor couldn't start his day until he drank several cups.

"Come with me to the break room and tell me what you found out." Joe took Ben's agreement for granted and headed through the silent office with quick, efficient steps.

The break room was deserted, setting the stage for Ben to tell his boss about Dr. Whitmore's role in his mother's death.

"I'd rather hear what's been happening around here first," Ben said.

Joe slanted him an understanding look, probably concluding Ben needed to work up the fortitude to discuss his mother. Was that the reason? Ben wondered.

"Okay, here's the rundown," Joe said under his breath, "This group-home story is kicking Larry's ass. You need to step in and show him how it's done."

A row of vending machines took up one wall of the austere, empty room. Joe headed straight for the contraption that dispensed coffee, putting an empty cup under the proper slot.

"I ran into Larry on my way in and that's not how it sounded to me," he said. "Larry said there's no story."

Joe jabbed the button that dispensed the coffee. Hard. "There's always a story. You know that."

Did he? Ben supposed that was an accurate description of his philosophy. But what if he came across a story where, using the group home director's words, the *greater good* wouldn't be served by going to press?

Joe handed Ben a full cup of black coffee then refilled his own while Ben sat down at the nearest table. Ben took a sip of the coffee, which left a bitter taste in his mouth.

"This is really bad stuff," he told Joe when his boss joined him.

"It's not the taste that's important. It's the caffeine." Joe took a healthy swallow. "Now here's what I want you to do. Talk to this director and the families of the people he booted, then work with Larry on writing the story."

"What if I agree there is no story?"

Joe snorted. "That'd be the day. You got to the bottom of who sent you that e-mail, didn't you?"

"Yeah, I did," Ben said slowly. "It was the granddaughter of a woman who'd worked as a nurse for Dr. Whitmore."

"So there was something there, just like you thought." Joe waited for him to elaborate.

There was no reason why he shouldn't. Dr. Whitmore had wronged his mother, then covered up the evidence. Ben had little doubt Joe would see the merits of publishing the piece: an investigative reporter's successful probe into his mother's death. The managing editor had suggested the angle himself.

Ben could envision the story running on the front page of the opinion section in a Sunday newspaper, where it would get the most readership. The wire services would probably pick it up. The weekly paper in Indigo Springs would run it.

"Well," Joe implored, "why did the nurse's granddaughter send the e-mail?"

Ben pictured Sierra's sad, lovely face when she'd told him what her father had done. He heard her voice quavering when she asked that he wait until after the festival to write the story.

She'd included her mother and brother when making the request, but he suspected it would be hardest for Sierra to deal with the publicity.

He swallowed. "The e-mail was a mistake. Dr. Whitmore acted as medical examiner after my mother died. The grandmother thought there was an irregularity with her blood sample, but there wasn't."

"So how did your mother die?"

"It happened just the way I was told." Ben thought he'd have difficulty with his next statement, but the words slipped off his tongue. "She died in an accident."

Joe nodded. He wouldn't have any reason to doubt

Ben's account. Nobody would. "You can still write the story if you like. Use the angle that sometimes things are exactly what they seem. It would still make a compelling piece."

"I'd rather not." Ben knew what had happened to his mother. He'd shared the news with his father and brothers by phone last night. All three had left it up to him whether to expose the late doctor's crime. Missy Cromartie wasn't interested in vengeance, either. She'd made it clear her objective was enlightening Allison Blaine's family about what her grandmother had witnessed.

"Fine with me." Joe took the news in stride. "So there's nothing stopping you from getting to work on that group home piece."

Nothing except a woman with huge, sad eyes who believed his need to expose the truth was greater than his feelings for her.

"Is it okay if that waits until Monday?" Ben asked, although the question was a formality. He couldn't work on the story when he wasn't in Pittsburgh. "I need some personal time."

"If you need until Monday," Joe said, "you need until Monday."

"Thanks." Ben drained the rest of his bad coffee and stood up, calling over his shoulder on his way out of the break room, "I'll see you Monday then."

"Hey," Joe's voice trailed him. "Where you going in such a hurry?"

Ben stopped only long enough to answer, "To do what I should have done days ago."

The right thing.

SIERRA STOOD BEHIND a table stacked with T-shirts in the tent that served as festival headquarters on Friday night. She'd been helping with T-shirt sales since getting off work even though she wasn't officially on the schedule until later in the weekend.

She needed to stay busy to keep her mind off the way her father had so grievously wronged the family of the man she loved. The man who had every reason to hate her father and think poorly of his daughter.

"What do you think?" Laurie Grieb held up a size XXL T-shirt in front of her, the voluminous material obscuring most of her body. "Is this the right size for when I start showing?"

"That's the right size if you're carrying quadruplets," Sara Brenneman quipped as she sank into a folding chair, the first time Sierra had seen her sit down tonight. The attorney was in charge of assuring that the festival's first day ran smoothly. With the last band getting set to play on the nearby stage, things were finally quieting down.

"Twins run in Kenny's family so you never know how many babies I'll have," Laurie said merrily as she handed over cash for the T-shirt. "And who knows. I might gain sixty pounds like my sister did when she got pregnant. Isn't that right, Sierra?"

Sierra dragged her mind away from Ben and made an attempt to smile. "I'd advise keeping the weight gain under sixty, but it can't hurt to buy clothes in a larger size."

"Oh, my gosh!" Laurie gasped and covered her mouth with both hands. "I just thought of something. My bridesmaid dress won't fit!"

"My wedding's not even two months away, and the dresses have empire waists," the attorney said. "You won't even be four months pregnant. You do not need a gigantic size bridesmaid dress."

"You don't know that." Laurie turned to Sierra. "Does she know that, Sierra?"

"Oh, no." Sierra put the double extralarge T-shirt in a bag and handed it to Laurie. "I am not, under any circumstances, disagreeing with the bride-to-be."

"I knew there was a reason I was really starting to like you," the attorney said to Sierra. "Now if only you could convince Laurie to start agreeing with me."

"Hey, I'm pregnant." Laurie placed her hands on her slender hips. "That gives me at least as much right as a bride-to-be to have people nod whenever I say anything."

Her friend and employer groaned. "This is going to be a long seven months."

"What's going to take seven months?" Annie entered the tent wearing a cute casual outfit Sierra had helped her pick out. The cropped green shirt matched her eyes, and the tight shorts that skimmed her knees highlighted her slender legs.

"My pregnancy," Laurie announced.

"And here I thought those things lasted nine." Annie's eyes sparkled. To the group, she said, "I love the band that's about to play. Ryan and I spread out a blanket in front of the stage so there's lots of room. Who wants to join us?"

"I do!" Laurie said. "Let me find Kenny and we'll be right there. You know what they say. It's never too early to introduce a baby to music."

She hurried off, leaving all three women smiling after her.

"You've been working all day, Sara. You go ahead and enjoy yourself," Sierra told the attorney. "I'll stay here."

"Are you sure?"

"Positive," Sierra said.

"It'll only be until someone comes by to help you pack up the T-shirts. We're storing them in an office nearby. Quincy said he'd round up someone to carry the boxes."

"I'll be waiting."

"You're a doll, Sierra." Sara turned to Annie. "I'll meet you out there. I roped in Michael to be a stage manager so it'll be just me. I'm going to check to make sure he's got things under control."

Annie hung back until the hospitality tent was empty except for her and Sierra. "Thanks again for stepping in for me on the committee," her sister-in-law said.

"No problem." Sierra smiled ruefully. "I'm glad to be busy this weekend. It gives me a legitimate reason to avoid my mother."

Rosemary Whitmore had turned deathly pale when Sierra confessed Ben knew everything, then walked away without a word. Annie and Ryan reacted much differently. They'd agreed Sierra had done the right thing, no matter how dire the consequences.

"So Rosemary still isn't talking to you?" Annie asked.

"Afraid not," Sierra said. "A little while ago, she pretended she didn't see me. She's pretty disappointed in me."

"You could be wrong about that," Annie said. "Last

night I came across her crying. At first I thought it was over your father, but she said she was sorry that poor woman had died. In her heart she knows what she convinced your father to do was wrong. She'll come around."

"She doesn't understand why I had to tell Ben everything," Sierra said.

"Did Ben understand?" Annie gazed at her through shrewd eyes. Her sister-in-law knew, Sierra thought. She knew Sierra loved Ben Nash.

"To Ben, I'm the daughter of the man who played a part in his mother's death," Sierra said sadly.

"I can't believe Ben thinks of you that way!"

"It's okay, Annie," Sierra said. "It's nothing less than I deserve."

A drumroll sounded outside the tent, followed by a voice over a microphone announcing the featured act of the evening.

"Get out of here, Annie," Sierra said. "That band you love is about to start."

It took some more convincing to get Annie to leave. When Sierra was alone, she stopped trying to put on a brave face. Despite what she'd told Annie, everything was not okay. The man she'd finally admitted she loved was about to have a story published that exposed her father's sin.

How could Ben not associate her with the man who might have contributed to his mother's death?

A shadow fell over her.

Her heart leaped, and her head jerked up. It was Chad Armstrong. Just as quickly, her heart plummeted in her chest. She felt silly for even thinking it might be

Ben, for harboring the hope he could look past what her father had done and come back to her.

She was clearly delusional.

"Quincy sent me to help with the T-shirts." Chad was wearing one of them, the aqua color a good match for his tan. She did a double take. Yes. His skin was lightly tanned, and his haircut was fresh and flattering. He'd always been thin, but his body looked more toned, as though he'd been working out.

"We sold so many today the overflow can fit in a couple boxes." She folded the garments and started packing them away. Chad pitched in.

"You avoided me at the committee meeting yesterday," he stated after a moment as they worked side by side.

That was true. She'd remembered his assertion that he needed to speak with her, but she hadn't been up to dealing with him.

"I've had a lot on my mind." She didn't owe him any more of an explanation than that.

He said nothing for what must have been a full minute while the rock music pulsed in the background. His voice was unemotional when he finally spoke. "You must know by now I want you back."

That was it. No apology for dumping her. No remorse for what he'd put her through.

"I figured as much." She folded another T-shirt. "The answer's no."

His lower lip thrust forward. Had he always sulked when he didn't get his way? "Does it have anything to do with that newspaper reporter?"

Her decision had everything to do with Ben, but not

in the way Chad meant. "Things didn't work out between Ben and me."

"Then why?"

"A lot of reasons. Number one being I'm no more suited for you than you are for me." Hadn't Ben pointed those facts out to her? Why had she argued with him when he'd been spot-on?

"That's not true," Chad protested. "We're perfect for each other. We went to high school together. We live in the same city. We both have good jobs. We want the same things out of life."

No, Sierra thought, *we don't.* Chad aimed to have the same kind of life her father had lived, a life that at one time Sierra had viewed as idyllic. She wanted something different. Instead of telling him any of that, Sierra said, "I'm sorry things didn't work out."

He nodded slowly. Sierra prepared for a rush of sadness that their years together were truly over, but it didn't come.

"I hope it's still okay for me to say a few words about your father at the park dedication on Sunday," Chad said. "You know how much I admired him."

Chad wouldn't think quite so highly of her father when word got out about Allison Blaine and the cover-up. As a pharmacist, Chad would recognize the gravity of her father's errors.

"There isn't going to be a dedication," Sierra said. "It was stricken from the festival lineup."

She hadn't filled Quincy Coleman in on all the details, simply relaying the *Pittsburgh Tribune* was about to publish a story casting her father in an unfavorable light.

"I heard about that," Chad said, "but you know it's back on the program, right?"

"That's impossible," she responded.

"I assure you it's not." Chad acted affronted that she'd question him. "I saw an updated schedule of events a short time ago."

"But…but how did that happen?"

"Nash might have had something to do with it," he said. "I overheard him talking to Quincy."

None of this made sense. She'd instituted the change to the lineup late yesterday. Ben had been back in Pittsburgh by then.

"When was this?" she asked. "Yesterday?"

"No," Chad said. "About an hour ago."

CHAPTER FOURTEEN

SIERRA SKIDDED to a stop after rushing out of the tent. A wall of people formed a perimeter around those sitting on blankets in front of the amphitheater.

She thought she'd mumbled an excuse to Chad for why she couldn't help him finish packing up the T-shirts.

She wouldn't swear to it, though.

She was only focused on finding out what Ben's presence in Indigo Springs meant.

The lead singer of the rock band let loose with a melodic howl. A guitar screeched, a drum beat out a frantic rhythm and then the four-member band really got going.

The music was so raucous Sierra could hardly think as she scanned the crowd for Ben. She spotted Jill Jacobi clapping her hands to the music on the edge of the crowd, her brother small and silent beside her. Sierra raised her vantage point, only seeking men over six feet tall.

Chase Bradford, a forest ranger who was a patient at Whitmore Family Practice, snuck a kiss from his girlfriend, Kelly. Nearby his father, Charlie, did a decidedly un-mayorlike dance for his laughing wife, Teresa.

A few other heads stuck out above the crowd, one of them female, most of them bobbing to the beat, none of them Ben's.

Maybe Chad had been mistaken about Ben's presence in Indigo Springs. As desperately as Sierra wanted to believe Ben was in town, what possible reason could he have to return to the place where his mother had so tragically died?

She crossed her arms over her chest and hugged herself, which was no comfort at all.

A hand touched the back of her right shoulder. She whipped her head around, then gazed up into dark, soulful eyes set in a lean, handsome face with the shadow of a beard.

The face of the man she loved.

"Ben." She said his name, although he couldn't possibly have heard her above the blaring rock music.

He moved his hand from her shoulder. Just when she thought he might let her go, he grabbed her hand.

"Let's get out of here," he said directly into her ear.

She nodded, breathing in the clean, familiar scent of him, uncaring of where they went. She'd follow him anywhere.

He didn't stick to Main Street, veering to a side street and walking purposefully away from the town center. She couldn't make any more sense of where he was leading her than why he'd returned.

When the music finally started to fade and a conversation would no longer involve shouting, Sierra asked him where they were going. It was far from the question she most wanted answered.

"You'll see in a minute," he said.

It took at least two. They walked without talking up and down one of the town's hilliest streets within a few blocks of where Sierra had grown up. The music became a distant murmur.

"This is it." He stopped in front of a modest, two-story house at the steep end of the street. If not for the porch light and the brightness of the moon, the place would be in complete darkness.

"Do you know the people who live here?" Sierra noted a lawn that needed mowing, the lack of cars in the driveway and a flyer hanging from the doorknob. The owners must be out of town.

"I used to know them," he said. "This was my grand-parents' house. It's where we stayed nineteen years ago."

She sucked in a breath, imagining the sad memories the house must invoke. "Is this the first time you've been back?"

"The second. I drove by earlier today." He jerked his head toward the rear of the house. "Come on. Let's trespass. I need to show you something."

She didn't hesitate, walking with him through the too-long grass, acutely aware of all the things they hadn't said, all the questions she'd yet to have answered.

The moon cast a soft, imperfect glow over a yard that sloped downward at a ninety-degree angle. Sierra was familiar enough with the geography of the area that she could envision the view from the house in daylight. A lush valley where pale pink mountain laurels grew in the springtime, the hillside leading to it dotted by houses.

"Since I found out my mom wanted to divorce my dad, I've been racking my brain to figure out why she let me believe we were only visiting," he said. "Then today, when I drove by this place, it hit me."

She didn't prompt him to continue when he paused. She sensed he needed to tell the story in his own time, in his own way.

"I had this memory of running down the hill over and over again, going faster and faster, challenging myself not to fall. I remember laughing even when I did fall, then getting up and doing it all over again."

He pointed to a deck that jutted out from the house and overlooked the yard.

"My mom and grandma were sitting up there, watching me. I could hear my grandma telling my mom to make me stop. There weren't any trees I could slam into or rocks where I could hit my head. But I was getting pretty dirty and banged up. I don't know why, but I remember the exact words my mother used. *Let him be happy.*" He paused in his narrative. "I think that's why she didn't tell me about the divorce."

Sierra digested his poignant tale, not completely sure she understood his conclusion. "Because she was protecting you?"

"Partly," Ben said. "But even more because she knew the truth would hurt and wanted to delay it as long as possible. I think it's the same reason she kept from me that she was pregnant with me when she got married."

"How do you feel about that?" she asked. "I know how important the truth is to you."

"It's still important," he said. "Otherwise, I wouldn't have come to Indigo Springs in the first place."

"Then clear something up for me." She was almost afraid to continue. "I heard a rumor you got the park dedication put back on the festival program."

"That's not a rumor."

"That doesn't make sense. When your story comes out, everyone will know what my father did."

"I'm not writing the story."

"But…but…" She couldn't form a coherent thought, couldn't understand why he'd pass up the opportunity to expose the facts. "What about the truth?"

"The truth is that ruining the reputation of a man who made a single mistake won't make me happy," he said. "When I told my editor there wasn't a story to write, I had the sense my mother would approve."

Sierra was afraid to believe what he was saying. "How about Missy Cromartie and the promise she made to her grandmother? Doesn't she want to see my father exposed?"

"I checked with Missy. She says her grandmother only wanted our family to know the truth of what happened to my mother. My dad and my brothers are fine with me not writing the story, too."

Sierra couldn't stop herself from asking the question. "How would they feel about a park being named for the man who covered up the circumstances of her death?"

"They had a tougher time with that one until I explained about you," Ben said. "They eventually understood your father did a lot of good with his life trying to make up for his mistake."

She wanted to make sure she'd heard correctly. "You told them about me?"

"I had to," he said. "They might not have heard me out if they didn't know I'm in love with Dr. Whitmore's daughter."

Her heart banged as forcefully as the drumming sound in the park. "You love me?"

"I thought that was obvious," he said. "There are a lot of reasons I'm not writing the story, but that's the main one."

"Because you love me," she repeated, this time in wonder.

He anchored his hands on her shoulders and met her eyes, the glowing moon revealing the sincerity shining in their depths. "I love you."

Joy soared inside her, but she was afraid to believe him. "You've only known me a week."

"Doesn't matter," he said. "You're in my heart to stay."

The darkness of the last few days disappeared, the brightness of their future so unexpected all she could do was gape at him.

"I'm coming on too strong, aren't I?" He grimaced. "You're right. We need time to get to know each other better. You can visit me in Pittsburgh, and I'll come see you in Indigo Springs."

"I'm not staying in Indigo Springs," she blurted out, surprising herself as much as him.

At his confused look, she continued, "I'm selling my half of the practice to Ryan. Family medicine isn't quite the right field for me. I think I might want to specialize in adolescents or work as a hospitalist."

"When did you decide that?"

"Just now," she admitted, although the plan sounded so right it must have been rattling around in her brain for months, if not years.

"Where are you going to relocate?"

"Pittsburgh, I think." She was coming up with the plan on the fly, yet nothing had ever made more sense. "Somebody recently told me it was a great place to live."

"You're moving to Pittsburgh?" Shock ran through his voice.

She nodded, more pleased with the strategy by the second. "You're the one who said I should live in a big city. Why not the place where you live?"

He felt his hands tighten on her shoulders and tension radiate through his body. "Are you sure? You grew up here. I know what I said, but the better I know you, the more I see how well you fit into the community."

"Only because you showed me there was more to life than work," Sierra said.

He felt his forehead furrow. "How did I do that?"

"By stirring things up," she said. "I would never have joined the festival committee if I wasn't trying to find out if Quincy Coleman sent you that e-mail. I was so busy acting like the perfect doctor I became every bit as dull as Chad said I was."

He thought of the woman who'd stripped for him,

fiercely defended her father and whooped it up at the arcade. "For the last time, you're not boring. You just got caught in the trap of acting…conservatively. The way you thought a doctor should act."

"I'm done with being conventional." She wound her arms around his neck. "I'm going to start taking chances right now."

"Oh, yeah." His mouth was just inches from hers, but he couldn't kiss her, not yet. What she had to say was too important. "What kind of chances?"

"I'm thinking about getting my hair cut really short."

He ran his fingers through the silken strands. "Okay, but you should know I love your hair just the way it is."

"You might be able to persuade me to keep it long then," she said, "considering I'm about to tell you I love you."

He grinned as joy swept over him. "That's not taking much of a chance considering you already know I love you back."

Her eyebrows arched. "I *am* moving to Pittsburgh."

"Now that is taking a chance." He moved his hands to the small of her back, enjoying the way she molded against him. She couldn't move to his city soon enough. "Since you're feeling risky, here's a suggestion. Get a place with a short-term lease. That way, you can move in with me when we know each other better."

Her upper teeth nibbled her lower lip. "What if I move in with you immediately?"

"You're serious?" He'd had the same thought, but hadn't wanted to push his luck. "You'd do that?"

"I do love you," she said. "And you did help me become a woman who takes chances."

He didn't reply. That was because she didn't give him the opportunity.

She kissed him.

And just like that, only one truth mattered. They were happy, and he planned to spend the rest of his life making damned sure they stayed that way.

* * * * *

Kay Young returned to woozy consciousness to find that she was lying on a soft sofa beneath a heap of quilts near a cheerfully burning fire. When she tried to move, however, everything hurt, and she groaned.

At once she heard a sound, then a stranger with a hard, harsh face was squatting beside her. "Shh," he said softly. "You're safe here. I promise."

"I have to go," she said weakly, struggling against pain. "He'll find me. He can't find me."

"Easy, lady," he said quietly. "You're hurt. No one's going to find you here."

"He will," she said desperately, terror clutching at her insides. "He always finds me!"

"Easy," he said again. "There's a blizzard outside. No one's getting here tonight, not even the doctor. I know, because I tried."

"Doctor? I don't need a doctor! I've got to get away."

"There's nowhere to go tonight," he said levelly. "And if I thought you could stand, I'd take you to a window and show you."

But even as she tried once more to pull away the quilts, she remembered something else: this man had been gentle when he'd found her beside the road, even when she had kicked and clawed. He hadn't hurt her.

Terror receded just a bit. She looked at him and detected signs of true concern there.

The terror eased another notch and she let her head sag on the pillow. "He always finds me," she whispered.

"Not here. Not tonight. That much I can guarantee."

*Will Kay's mysterious rescuer protect
her from her worst fears?
Find out in HER HERO IN HIDING by*
New York Times *bestselling author Rachel Lee.
Available June 2010, only from
Silhouette® Romantic Suspense.*

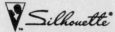

ROMANTIC
SUSPENSE

Sparked by Danger, Fueled by Passion.

NEW YORK TIMES AND *USA TODAY*
BESTSELLING AUTHOR

RACHEL LEE

BRINGS YOU AN ALL-NEW
CONARD COUNTY: THE NEXT GENERATION SAGA!

After finding the injured Kay Young on a deserted country
road Clint Ardmore learns that she is not only being hunted
by a serial killer, but is also three months pregnant.
He is determined to protect them—even if it means
forgoing the solitude that he has come to appreciate.
But will Clint grow fond of having an attractive woman
occupy his otherwise empty ranch?

Find out in

Her Hero in Hiding

Available June 2010 wherever books are sold.

Visit Silhouette Books at www.eHarlequin.com

SRS27681

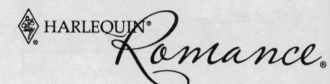

Four friends, four dream weddings!

On a girly weekend in Las Vegas, best friends Alex, Molly,
Serena and Jayne are supposed to just have fun and forget
men, but they end up meeting their perfect matches!
Will the love they find in Vegas stay in Vegas?

Find out in this sassy, fun and wildly romantic miniseries
all about love and friendship!

Saving Cinderella! by MYRNA MACKENZIE
Available June

Vegas Pregnancy Surprise by SHIRLEY JUMP
Available July

Inconveniently Wed! by JACKIE BRAUN
Available August

Wedding Date with the Best Man
by MELISSA MCCLONE
Available September

Love Inspired®

Bestselling author

JILLIAN HART

brings you another heartwarming story
from

GRANGER FAMILY RANCH

Rancher Justin Granger hasn't seen his high school sweetheart
since she rode out of town with his heart. Now she's back, with
sadness in her eyes, seeking a job as his cook and housekeeper.
He agrees but is determined to avoid her...until he discovers
that her big dream has always been him!

The Rancher's Promise

*Available June
wherever books are sold.*

Steeple
Hill®
LI87601

www.SteepleHill.com

REQUEST YOUR FREE BOOKS!
2 FREE NOVELS PLUS 2 FREE GIFTS!

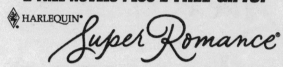

HARLEQUIN®
Super Romance®

Exciting, emotional, unexpected!

YES! Please send me 2 FREE Harlequin® Superromance® novels and my 2 FREE gifts (gifts are worth about $10). After receiving them, if I don't wish to receive any more books, I can return the shipping statement marked "cancel." If I don't cancel, I will receive 6 brand-new novels every month and be billed just $4.69 per book in the U.S. or $5.24 per book in Canada. That's a saving of at least 15% off the cover price! It's quite a bargain! Shipping and handling is just 50¢ per book.* I understand that accepting the 2 free books and gifts places me under no obligation to buy anything. I can always return a shipment and cancel at any time. Even if I never buy another book from Harlequin, the two free books and gifts are mine to keep forever.

135/336 HDN E5P4

Name _____ (PLEASE PRINT) _____

Address _____ Apt. #

City _____ State/Prov. _____ Zip/Postal Code

Signature (if under 18, a parent or guardian must sign)

Mail to the **Harlequin Reader Service:**
IN U.S.A.: P.O. Box 1867, Buffalo, NY 14240-1867
IN CANADA: P.O. Box 609, Fort Erie, Ontario L2A 5X3

Not valid for current subscribers to Harlequin Superromance books.
**Are you a current subscriber to Harlequin Superromance books
and want to receive the larger-print edition?
Call 1-800-873-8635 today!**

* Terms and prices subject to change without notice. Prices do not include applicable taxes. N.Y. residents add applicable sales tax. Canadian residents will be charged applicable provincial taxes and GST. Offer not valid in Quebec. This offer is limited to one order per household. All orders subject to approval. Credit or debit balances in a customer's account(s) may be offset by any other outstanding balance owed by or to the customer. Please allow 4 to 6 weeks for delivery. Offer available while quantities last.

Your Privacy: Harlequin Books is committed to protecting your privacy. Our Privacy Policy is available online at www.eHarlequin.com or upon request from the Reader Service. From time to time we make our lists of customers available to reputable third parties who may have a product or service of interest to you. If you would prefer we not share your name and address, please check here. ☐

Help us get it right—We strive for accurate, respectful and relevant communications. To clarify or modify your communication preferences, visit us at www.ReaderService.com/consumerschoice.

HSR10R

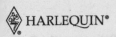

HARLEQUIN®

Showcase

On sale May 11, 2010

Reader favorites from the most talented voices in romance

Save $1.00 on the purchase of 1 or more Harlequin® Showcase books.

SAVE $1.00 on the purchase of 1 or more Harlequin® Showcase books.

Coupon expires Oct 31, 2010. Redeemable at participating retail outlets.
Limit one coupon per purchase. Valid in the U.S.A. and Canada only.

52609015

65373 00076 2   (8100)0 11651

® and TM are trademarks owned and used by the trademark owner and/or its licensee.
© 2009 Harlequin Enterprises Limited

HSCCOUP0410

COMING NEXT MONTH

Available June 8, 2010